HOGBACK

Raland J. Patterson

Bloomington, IN Milton Keynes, UK

authorHOUSE™

AuthorHouse™
1663 Liberty Drive, Suite 200
Bloomington, IN 47403
www.authorhouse.com
Phone: 1-800-839-8640

AuthorHouse™ UK Ltd.
500 Avebury Boulevard
Central Milton Keynes, MK9 2BE
www.authorhouse.co.uk
Phone: 08001974150

First published by AuthorHouse 6/22/2006

ISBN: 1-4259-4353-5 (sc)
ISBN: 1-4259-4354-3 (dj)

Printed in the United States of America
Bloomington, Indiana

This book is printed on acid-free paper.

Table of Contents

War! 1

The Setup 9

A New Town 13

A New Job 21

New Friends 25

The Mission 31

A Lady 37

Michael & Susan 39

The Plan 45

Big Red Foster 51

Woman Killer 57

The Hunter 63

Finding Magic 73

Mr. Bob & Craig Foster 79

Equipment 83

Falling in Love 87

Getting Ready 93

A Good Place to Live 97

The Picnic 99

Finding the Equipment 105

Romantic Plans 109

A Hunting Trip 113

Special Night.. 123

The Letter 129

Billy Bob's Missing... 135

Fire Department... 141

A Phone Call 145

The Requirements 147

A Failed Test 149

Peggy's Surprise.. 153

The Phone Call.. 157

The Second Letter 161

Bob's First Pain 163

Following the Plan 167

Thanksgiving Dinner 169

A Planned Separation 173

Sam McGill 175

The Final Phrase... 179

The Scoutmaster.. 183

Dress Rehearsal 187

The Shot... 191

Peggy's Home... 195

The Airport 199

San Francisco 201

A Surprise 207

Return to Blue Ridge 209

Reviewing the Past 211

Getting Settled... 215

First Visit With Peggy 219

Planning A Wedding..223

Getting the License 225

Getting Married...231

Married...235

Complete Truth 237

Getting Help..243

Jail Visit 249

The Hospital 251

Good News...257

Baby's New Home..263

New Postal Worker 267

Execution Postponed 271

Brotherhood..273

The Rifles...277

The Pardon...279

1

War!

CW3 MICHAEL BARKLEY ARRIVED AT the darkest part of the parking area to brief his flight crew on the day's mission, copilot CW2 Jeff Larson, crew chief SP4 Roy Barnes, and door gunner Charlie Jones. "Chief, why did you let your pilot put you here, in this position?"

"He knew this was not his bird today so he didn't look for a better location."

"I'll do better tonight. This has got to be the worst place on the airfield. You can't get here without wading mud holes. It's so quiet it makes me feel like I'm in a graveyard."

"It does feel weird. Why don't you give us the briefing so we can leave."

"Roger that," Barkley said. "It looks like we'll get some sun today. Our mission for the next few days is to fly to Nancy and be on call for COL Gray. We're stuck with the commo bird. Chief, you and Jonsey need to take your tools."

1

"Why's that, sir?"

"I thought you could take care of the scheduled inspection while we wait. Or do you want to do them after we get back at night?"

"Thanks, sir. Were you a crew chief before you went to flight school?"

"Yes, why?"

"Because the other pilots wouldn't care if Jonsey and I work late or not. Thanks."

Jeff asked, "Why don't we just standby here and save flight hours?"

"It's a status thing. COL Gray likes having his own helicopter at his beck and call."

"What an asshole. All I can say is 21 and a wakeup!"

"Jeff, did you take care of the preflight?"

"It's done. What about all of that radio equipment in the back?"

"It's okay. We won't be using it today."

"It sure takes up a lot of room. How did we get stuck with it?"

"Battalion has a big mission near Cambodia and they need all the birds they can get."

"Yeah, you sure can't haul troops in *Old Paint.*"

"Watch it or you'll hurt her feelings."

"Yeah. She can't help it they put that big radio console on her."

"She can handle a brigade exercise with all those radios back there."

"Jonsey get those C-rations loaded," Barkley said. "We can't be late to our first day of leisure. Chief, untie the rotor blade."

"Roger that!"

"All clear?"

"Clear!"

"Coming hot."

"Everything looks good. Let's go to Nancy!"

"Tower, this is Army 685. Request hover and departure to the south."

"Good morning, 685. No other traffic. You are cleared direct."

"Thanks much! On the go!"

"God, I love to fly this time of day. The air is so smooth."

"Me, too. Bet we won't fly this early in the states."

"I'm sure. Chief, hand Jeff the logbook and let's get the DER (an in-flight check on the engine; the maintenance officer would plot the engine temperature looking for a rise; in 1969 a helicopter's engine life was about 500 hours; usually the temperature would start creeping up just before engine failure) check out of the way."

"You got a pencil?"

"Gee whiz! You're the only pilot I know that doesn't carry a pencil! Give me the book. You fly. I'll write."

"I've got the bird."

"You've got it."

"It's looking like I really need to slow the airspeed down to hold the altitude."

"That's okay, just another 30 seconds and I'll have it. Got it."

"Good. Let's get down to fifty feet where it's safe."

"Is that a short-timer talking?"

"No reason to do dumb things now."

"I guess. Come up on Victor (VHF Radio) and let's see if any other killer spades are out there."

"On Victor. Good Morning, Vietnam!"

"Hey, is that the short-timer bird talking?"

"That's me."

"How many 'til you get on the freedom bird?"

"Seventeen and wake up."

"Where are you going?"

"Firebase Nancy."

"Oh. Looks like CPT Wright is taking care of his pets."

"Yeah. He wants us to get good tans before we leave country. Where are you guys going?"

"Me and Savage are resupplyin' the recon team we dropped in three days ago."

"Dennis, ask Savage if he's shot any more holes in the water tank."

"Go to hell, Michael! You know Panther bet me that my .357 couldn't make a hole in that steel. I showed him!"

"Yeah. We didn't have water for two days! Boy, the old man was pissed about that! Dennis, the DER done yet?"

"Oh my, God no! CPT White told me if I missed it one more time he would kick my ass! I think he meant it, too. Talk to you when we finish. Out."

"Mayday, Mayday! This is Army copter 781 going down, grid 6434—grid 6434!"

"Jeff, that sounds like Dennis. Come up on Victor and find out.

"Savage is that you with the Mayday?"

"Yeah, Dennis is on guard."

"What happened?"

"When we were doing our check, a Quad 50 put a round through our engine. Dennis is trying to make the only clearing we can see."

"Come up on Company FOX MIKE radio and we'll home in on you."

"Thanks, buddy."

"Jeff, give COL Gray a call at Nancy and tell him we're assisting a bird down."

"Roger that."

"Savage, how many on board, over?"

"Eight, counting crew."

"Mike, COL Gray wants to know why Med Evac can't handle it? He wants his aircraft. He might want to go somewhere later."

"Tell him it'll take Med Evac thirty minutes before they get here. It's a hot LZ and they need help now."

"I'll tell him, but he won't be happy. Know what I mean—"

"Who cares? If we don't go get 'em, Charlie will."

"I agree. Let's do it!"

A few minutes later Michael announced, "Nearly there. Keep your eyes open! Does anyone see them?"

The gunner screamed, "There they are! Eleven o'clock, next to that big crater."

"Savage, we have you in sight!"

"It's about time! We're taking small arms fire from the north tree line."

"Gunner! Spray the friggin' tree line. Keep their heads down."

"Savage! Looks like Dennis picked the only good spot to land. We'll try landing about fifty feet behind you. That's about as close as we can get. Tell Dennis we've got the commo bird today. Only room for 4 paxs at most."

"We understand—no room! We've got two guys that're hit! We'll send them first!"

"Send 'em on back! We'll take them to Nancy and come back for you guys."

Looking around quickly, Mike saw an eerie sight. The morning sun had created patches of ground fog about three to four feet deep. The burnt stumps and snags made it look like a horror movie.

Suddenly from his right, his eyes tracked incoming tracer fire. It was the first time he had tasted fear like this since he'd been in 'Nam. Knowing he could ill afford to lose his nerve, he reminded himself he had a job to do. People's lives depended on him keeping his head and making sound decisions.

"Jeff, we're sitting ducks! Chief, help 'em! We've got to get out of here!"

"Chief, we loaded yet?"

"We are now!"

Pulling pitch, Michael announced hard," We're on the go! Savage! Keep your head down for the next thirty minutes. I'll be back to get you!"

"Can you bring a cheese sandwich?"

"White or wheat?"

"You decide!"

Michael pulled max power, keeping the nose down to pick up as much airspeed as he could before getting to the tree line. Once there he eased back on the cycle and quickly climbed over the trees. "Jeff, flying's right up there with sex, man!"

"Boy, do you need to see Susan!"

"Seventeen and a wakeup!"

As the copter departed the LZ, the crew encountered increased gunfire.

"Jeff, call Nancy and have the medics waiting at the pad. Chief how bad are they hit?"

"One in the leg, not bad, the other, in the chest. Looks real bad."

"The medics are already at the pad. The Med Evac is almost here. The colonel wants to know if you want them to go to Nancy or the downed aircraft?"

"Tell him all the wounded will be at Nancy. We'll head back and pick up the rest."

"Guys, I only want to be on the ground for thirty seconds, that's it, so move it. When we get there help get these wounded off. Savage and Dennis need our help now!"

Thirty seconds after the skids hit the pad, Jeff announced hard, "They are off and we're clear!"

Michael pulled pitch, nose down flying only inches above the ground. He quickly hit 90 knots then climbed to twenty feet above the trees. Seeing the flight level, Jeff said, "Can we fly a little lower?"

"Now remember we're short."

"Oh, yeah. What was I thinking?"

Five minutes out, Michael called the downed crew. "Savage! You still there?"

"Yeah! What's taking so long?"

"We thought we'd toast your sandwich first. Don't worry. We're three minutes out. Status? How hot is it?"

"I think they brought in their relatives. Your best approach is from the south. Stay away from the rubber plantation. The Quad 50 is there."

"Roger that. Getting closer to the deck."

"Yeah, sweet music, I can hear you. Can you land a little closer this time? We've got to carry these M-60s out."

"Can you destroy the machines guns?"

"No."

"Okay, we'll try getting closer. Geez! Looks bad down there!"

"Yeah. That napalm leaves a lot of snags and trees. You'd think they were fighting a war or something."

"How about that crater on your right front? Can we land there?"

"Yeah. Just watch that stump on our side."

"Get everything! I'm not coming back."

"Roger that."

Thirty seconds on the ground turned into three minutes and seemed a lifetime for the crew. Michael watched as carefully as he could the activity around him. It seemed that every one was moving in slow motion. Even the enemy's rifle fire striking the ground around them created slow moving clouds of dust. A smile came over Michael's face when he thought this was like watching a 3-D movie—a lot of action with no one really getting hurt. Then a cold chill hit every fiber in his body—this was not a movie and people could die. All he could think about was putting the power to the blades to get out! "Jeff, for chrissakes, how much longer?"

"Everyone's on board! Let's go!"

"The wind's picked up! I'm going to fly low-level crosswind as long as I can then turn into the wind. That's the only way we can keep from over flying those guns."

"I agree. Go for it!"

As he pulled pitch, the ground fire intensified.

"Guys, we're taking fire from the tree line—two o'clock! Gunners! Hit 'em! Just a little more and we'll be gone!"

Suddenly blood sprayed on Jeff's arm and leg but he felt no pain. He turned to see that the blood came from Michael. He tried to take control of the aircraft. "I've got the aircraft." Jeff screamed, "I've got the aircraft! Michael! Michael, you've been hit! Let go of the damned cycle. I've got the aircraft!"

Michael could only click his mike.

"Chief! Michael's been hit! Move up here and tilt his seat back so you can see how bad it is!"

The others in the rear could see what was going on. They quickly flipped Michael's seat back and took off his flak jacket. Then Dennis turned on his mike, "He's been hit in the neck just above his chicken plate. He's bleeding badly. You've gotta get him to a hospital now!"

"On Guard, Med Evac bird, this is 685, fifteen minutes north of Nancy"

"685, this is Med Evac. We're just leaving Nancy."

"This is 685, my pilot has been hit, bad. Where's the nearest Doctor?"

"685 that's where we're going. Tune your Fox Mike to 54 38. I'll give you a long count, just home in us and we'll lead you there."

"Roger 54 38."

Then Dennis yelled, "It's too late Jeff— Michael's dead!"

2
The Setup

"Sonny, I told ya those college girls weren't gonna have anything to do with us."

"Yeah…well, Tim, if you'da kept yer mouth shut, they woulda never known."

"Sorry. She just caught me off guard when she asked what I was majorin' in, and it sorta just slipped out."

"A shame. They drank half our beer but loved my birthday present from Daddy."

"Big surprise— Who wouldn't love a candy red T-Bird?"

"Gimme another beer."

"Last two, man. Told you a case of suds wouldn't last all day. I've got a wonderful buzz goin' and the night's young."

"Let's get some more. Sound like a plan?"

"A, whoa… Nobody's gonna sell us beer here in Athens. Let's get another case from your Dad's basement."

"Why don't you time us, huh? Let's see a new record back to Washington."

"You're on. But remember…you need to slow down in Lexington."

"Yeah, for sure. Deputy Fife thinks he's Buford T. Justice."

As they left Lexington, Sonny asked, "How's our time?"

No answer.

"Tim! How are we doing? Are you asleep?" *Jesus, he's passed out*, Sonny said to himself. *Great! Well, I wanted to go see Bonnie anyway.*

Realizing there was no reason to slow down so close to home, he stepped on the accelerator and watched for any intruding traffic on the side streets. His attention riveted the new sign for the Washington Apple Orchard. When his eyes again concentrated on the road his headlights caught a glimpse of something in his lane. Swerving to miss the uncertain object without any concern for his own safety, the car fishtailed and almost rolled over. He then realized, *Oh my God! It was a bicycle!*

The bike and rider had hit the side of his car, bouncing them hard into the ditch. He quickly stopped and ran to see what could be done. It was a little girl on a bicycle, the bent frame now wrapped around her legs. He knew it must be painful. He knew too he shouldn't move her.

He climbed the bank on the other side of the ditch and slid down slowly to see if he could help, while, of course, not moving her. When in position, he saw a most gruesome sight, as half of her face was missing. He vomited uncontrollably at what lie before him. Without warning, his knees gave way and he collapsed unconscious in the ditch next to her still body.

Out cold for a good thirty minutes, he staggered back to the car, no longer drunk just scared. He screamed out loud, "What I'm going to do? I've got to find Daddy! Daddy will know what to do, but first I've got to take Tim home. Thank heaven, Tim is still out of it and doesn't have a clue."

He drove to Tim's house and parked in the street, quickly got out and made it to the passenger side of the car, opened the door and shook Tim from side to side.

"Wake up! Come on, wake up! Get out. I'm going to Bonnie's—"

"What about the beer?" Tim managed to say.

"We'll get it tomorrow. Hit the rack and go to sleep."

"Okay— Twist my arm..."

Sonny drove home as quickly as he could without breaking any speed laws or doing anything reckless that might cause a policeman to look his way. He got home safely, ran into the house and flipped the light on in his Dad's bedroom without any concern for the time of night. "Daddy! I'm in trouble."

His father took a few moments to come to the surface, realized it was his son, then reacted to the strong light and covered his eyes with his hand and said, "What? What time is it? What are you talking about?"

"I hit a little girl on a bicycle with my car."

"How bad is it?"

"I...I think she's dead."

"Dead? Oh, my God! Go down to the living room and call Woodrow."

"Our lawyer?"

"Yeah. Who do you think is going to get you out of this mess? Tell him to get his ass over here right now."

"Where did it happen? Were you by yourself?"

"In front of Washington's Apple Orchard. Tim was with me but he had two sheets to the wind from the beer and didn't see a thing."

"Where is he now?"

"I took him home and told him I was going to pick up Bonnie for a late date."

"Good idea."

"Is the car damaged?" Sonny's father said.

"I'm not sure."

"Well, let's go look."

While they checked out the car in the garage, the lawyer drove up, cut his lights before coming to a stop and quietly got out and walked to the garage side entrance, lighted by the fluorescents inside, and stepped in. "What's so important?"

"Sonny had an accident. He hit a little girl in Washington and we think he may have killed her. What can you do?"

"Did anybody see it?"

"I don't think so," Sonny chimed in. "Tim was with me but he was out cold, Bud Light."

"That's good. What we need to do is find somebody to take the blame, otherwise the police are like hound dogs over an open case file."

Boss Carter asked, "Anyone in mind?"

"No. Do you?"

"What about that drunk that has the son who's always in trouble?" Carter said.

"Coleman?"

"Yeah. That's his name."

"Does he still gamble a lot?"

"Yeah. I think he owes most everyone in the county."

"Tomorrow go get all those markers and bring Mr. Coleman to my house. Sonny, you go pick up the teenager, nice and friendly like, let him drive your car around town, the hamburger joints and all."

"My new car?"

"Yes, your new car. The one you killed the girl with, ah, dah! We need his fingerprints in the car, thank you very much. If we are going to get you out of trouble, you are going to have to do as I say. Understand?"

"Yes, Daddy."

3

A New Town

August, 1976, Blue Ridge, GA

THE TRAILWAYS BUS STOPPED IN front of the terminal and a tall, slender man stepped down to the sidewalk. Looking up the street, he commented to the driver, "I have never seen a bus station next to the City Hall and jail before."

"Convenient, I guess," replied the driver. "That's Billy Bob Foster's world. You need to steer clear of him. Real clear."

"How's that?"

"He's the town sheriff and likes doing his job, if you know what I mean."

The man looked around and then asked where he could get something to eat. The driver told him, "If you just want a snack, the Rexall Drug Store is just around the corner. If you are looking for the best hamburger in town, just walk down Main until you reach Hall Street. Turn left, go one block and you'll see the Tastee Freeze on the right. It's where most of the teenagers hang out. If heaven doesn't have burgers like that, it might be worth stayin' here—"

He thanked the driver and began to walk and it wasn't long before he began to question the bus driver's directions. He became concerned when he started down the street and it looked like a residential area with big houses that must have been built at the turn of the century. He made a left and began to walk straight up a hill, houses still on both sides of the street. At the top of the hill he came to First Street, which looked more like a highway. It appeared to be the main thoroughfare through town bypassing the downtown business section. He looked right and, sure enough, there was the Tastee Freeze on the other side of the highway, about a half block away. He picked up his pace. The long bus ride from Atlanta had made him hungry.

He walked though the parking area and realized it was like all the old curb service hamburger shops, circa 1950s. Two waitresses, or as they were called, carhops, were taking care of all the cars as they came in. One of the carhops was a pretty blond and every boy in the place wanted her to wait on his car. Jim thought the world never changes, at least down South anyway.

He walked through the front door and took the first empty booth on the right, which seemed rather strange, as the place was really crowded. After a few moments, a tall brunette appeared and said, "What can I get for you?"

"A large Coke, two hamburgers medium well and fries, plenty of catsup."

"Coming up! Do you want those served to you here?"

"Yes, why not?"

"You'll see," she replied with a chuckle as she walked off. He relaxed and began to look around. He thought to himself, *The South never changes. If the small towns could just get rid of the power-hungry parasites, the South would be heaven on earth.*

As he was enjoying his surroundings, a couple of teenagers came up to the jukebox. They had pooled their money so they could get the maximum number of songs. Everyone was calling out his or her choice. He thought, *Normal as normal can be.* When the first record began to play he quickly realized why no one wanted the booth. The teenagers in the back of the room watched his reaction. He seemed to meet their expectations because they began to laugh enthusiastically.

An older woman who appeared to be the owner came over and did something to the back of the jukebox and the music quieted down. "Sorry about that. The kids today want to *feel* the music, not just listen to it. Normally I don't care, as it's just them that suffer. That wall over there protects me and m' cooks. Goes without sayin' you're not from around here."

"I just arrived in town an hour ago on the bus from Atlanta."

"You got family here?"

"No, I'm not even sure I'm in the right place."

"The right place? How's that?"

"A friend of mine told me about a small town near here where everything is owned by one family. He said the family wasn't liked much; however, they provided the jobs and no one openly complained. I need a job. I hope I'm in the right place."

"Mister, you've described Blue Ridge to a T. You are talking about the Foster family. Foster's Lumber Mill employs over half the town. The Fosters also own or are part owners of the bank, department store and most other business in the county. About the only thing they don't control is the post office. Sandy, the lady waiting on you, has a husband who used to work at the mill in Ellijay, 'til his accident anyway."

"Wait— Thought you said the Fosters were in *this* town."

"They are. The Foster's mansion takes up the whole block just across from Hackney's Cleaners. Can't miss it. I'm Bonnie by the way. This is my place."

"I'm Jim Cole. Nice to meet you."

"Well, Jim, hope to see more of you. I need the business, Lord knows. These teenagers are great but they are always *low on funds* you might say."

"Thanks for turning down the jukebox."

"Don't mention it. I was just looking for an excuse. Your predicament gave me one."

I found my town, Jim said to himself. *Now I need to find a job and my targets.*

The waitress brought his Coke and food. "Anything else, mister?"

"Yes, could I have some ketchup?"

"Oh, sorry about that. These kids keep stealing the bottle off the table because no one usually sits here."

"And now I know why! I'm Jim Cole. Bonnie said your name was Sandy. Is that right?"

"Yes, sir. Nice to meet you, Jim. She told me you had just arrived from Atlanta. Good place to be from. Can't stand large cities."

"Oh, Atlanta's not bad, depending."

"Well, you seem to be at home in this one-horse town for whoever knows why."

Smiling, Cole said, "I should be. I was raised in one just like it next to the South Carolina border. We even had a single family there that owned the town. Nothing much has changed in this world. The family in my town was the Carters. My town was a little different, though. The Carter family had a son that Boss Carter doted over. Sonny was his name and as far as the Boss and the law were concerned he could do no wrong."

"In this town his name is Craig, Mr. Bob's pride and joy. Sorta thinks of himself as a ladies man. Mr. Bob brags he probably has more grandchildren than anyone in the county." Laughing, to herself, she admitted out loud there seemed to be an increase in the number of red-headed children in the past five years or so.

"Bonnie said Mr. Bob doesn't control the post office. Do you think I could get a job there?"

"Dunno, it's run by Mike and Mother Barkley. They're getting up in years and could use the help, sure enough. They always stop by on their way home. Mother Barkley doesn't cook much anymore. The Barkleys treat us like family. You cannot help but like them. If you are still here, I can introduce you if you like. Oh! I just had a thought. I just met you! You seem nice enough. You're not a killer or anything, are you?"

"Not really. I only kill people that need killing."

"Like a soldier?"

"Yes, exactly." That explanation seemed sufficient.

A while later the Barkleys showed up. Sandy did her cordial best—"Jim Cole, it was Cole wasn't it?"

"Yes, Cole. Jim Cole."

"Mr. Jim Cole, this is Mr. and Mrs. Barkley. Jim came in on the afternoon bus from Atlanta and is looking for a job in the post office. Do you think you can help him?"

"I think we just might. We do need some help. Have you ever worked in a post office before?"

"Yes sir, a couple of summers when I was in high school. That's why I mentioned to Sandy that I'd be interested in any opening you might have. That's how I earned my spending money. I worked part time, never took a test for the position or anything."

"Well," said Mr. Barkley, "my missus and I are gettin' a might slow. I didn't say old, just slow. We could use some part-time help. I'm afraid the pay's not much. We can only afford minimum wage. If you have a skill, Mr. Bob could put you on at the mill for twice that amount."

"Sir, I have always loved post office work. I have a few dollars saved from an inheritance and as long as the money lasts I would like to work a job I enjoy. When can I start?"

"Why, I guess tomorrow at 7:00 a.m.!"

"Can you tell me where I can get a room—a room that a minimum wage employee can afford?"

Mrs. Barkley looked at her husband and they both turned to Jim and together announced, "If you don't mind doing a little work on the premises, there's a small apartment over the post office, hasn't been used in years. Not since our son went off to Vietnam. Did you go to Vietnam?"

"No, I wanted to but was too young at the time."

"Our son was a helicopter pilot with the First Cavalry Division. He was killed two weeks before he was to return home. Jeff Larson, one of his soldier friends, came by to see us a few years ago. He said Michael was killed while trying to rescue another helicopter crew. Jeff said it was someone else's job to rescue them but they were in trouble so Michael went to help. Michael was always like that, helpin' others and all. Jeff said eight men owe their lives to him. He earned a Silver Star and a Purple Heart. They say he was a hero. We're so proud of him."

"You should be. You raised a wonderful son."

"Thank you! We've always thought so!"

"Mr. Barkley, would it be imposing if I asked to see the apartment tonight?"

"Why no. It wouldn't," Mr. Barkley said, "Sandy, can we have our soup to go? We need to take Jim to his new home."

"His new home?"

"Yes, it's about time we let someone move into Michael's apartment."

"Well, Mr. Jim Cole," Sandy said, "you've been in town less than four hours and you already have a job and an apartment. Do you always move so fast?"

"Not really. I guess you're my lucky charm."

The Barkleys moved around the apartment and touched the contents with a reverence that came from a long, lost love remembered. Mrs. Barkley suddenly stopped and with tears in her eyes apologized that they should have moved their son's things years ago. He felt guilty that he was putting the kind couple through this emotional roller coaster. They reminded him of his own grandparents who, in his mind, were the only couple he ever knew that was truly in love. They shared a love that he felt only existed in love stories. His grandparents loved each other to the end. Mamaw died at the age of 85 and Papaw the day after her funeral. It was strange he hadn't thought of his grandparents in years. In fact, not since they came to the county jail when he was transferred to the prison for boys. They were the only family members to provide him support at the trial. They were unaware he had been set up by his own father to be punished for something he had not done. They loved him with a nonjudgmental love that only came with true love. Jim knew now he had made it easy for his father and the court by his foolish actions as a teenager. He should have listened to his sister and mom. *That was then and this is now,* he thought. Boss Carter was in charge then and since his release five years ago Jim Cole took charge and if he played his cards right he should make a wonderful career out of being in charge.

Eventually, Mrs. Barkley found a box and began to put Michael's things into it. After a few rushed minutes she had removed the little things that had made the room Michael's. Mr. Barkley told him to feel free to move anything around and if he did not want something to just place it in the storage shed out back. "Here's the key. There is nothing of value in it except Michael's Army bag we received after his death."

Seeing that the visit to the room was very hard on his wife, he looked at Jim and gave him a little wink. Turning to his wife, "Mother, let's get out of here and let Jim get some sleep. He has a tough day tomorrow with a tough boss."

Jim sat on the bed after the Barkleys left and got into a funk about whether he might have found a town that would force him to adjust his mission in life. *Tomorrow will tell,* he thought. *Tomorrow will tell.*

4
A New Job

NEXT MORNING JIM WAITED AT the front door of the post office. Because there had been no water in the apartment, he was forced to use the restroom of the service station across the railroad tracks to wash up and shave. Not used to shaving in cold water, he cut himself several times and stopped the bleeding by putting little pieces of toilet paper on the cuts. When Mr. Barkley saw him, he began to laugh at the top of his lungs, so long and hard he had to sit down. When he just kept laughing, Jim and Mrs. Barkley began to laugh as well. The people in the shop next door came out to see what the noise was all about. The shop owner said, "Mike, what is all the laughing about?"

Mr. Barkley pointed to Jim, "Do you remember the first time Michael tried to use my straight razor? I don't know who got cut the most, Michael then or Jim now!"

The shop owner responded, "Mike, it's great to hear that big laugh of yours. The whole town has missed it."

Mike Barkley turned to Jim, "What did you do to yourself?"

"There was no water in the apartment and I had to use the service station down the street. It's been quite a few years since I shaved with cold water. I had forgot that it makes a difference."

"Well, we've got to do something about that. Come on back to the rear of the post office and let's turn on the water valve for the apartment. Other than no water how did you sleep in your new home?"

"Great, you and Mrs. Barkley have been too kind."

"Nonsense, my boy! I haven't seen a gleam in Mother's eyes since we lost Michael. We should be thanking you! You have a home as long as you want it."

Mr. and Mrs. Barkley were making it even harder to remember why he came here in the first place. Could this be a stopping point; a new life for Jim Coleman, known as Jim Cole? Time would tell. He was right.

As each day went by, he felt more at home. His first payday came and the new money was burning a hole in his pocket. He felt he could waste it on a good time, after all, the job at the post office was not why he came to town.

As he swept out the lobby of the post office, Sandy, from the Tastee Freeze, appeared with a need to buy stamps.

"Well, if it isn't old fast mover."

"Well, if it isn't my lucky charm. Maybe you can tell me where a young, single man with money in his pocket can go to have fun."

"That would be the Supper Club."

"I can't afford a club."

"No, silly. It's just a bar with dancing. It's located just outside of town on the other side of the county line. Fannin County is dry— which means no beer. Gilmer County is wet. It's just called a club instead of a bar. That's the way Mr. Bob wants it. The talk is that Mr. Bob is a silent partner and that's why he will not let Fannin County sell booze. If you go, be careful. You do not want to drive by the Blue Ridge city limit sign. That's where Mr. Bob's city sheriff, Billy Bob, waits to give out tickets."

"I can't drive as I don't have car or a license."

"Then don't walk down the highway near the sign either. Billy Bob will get you for disturbing the peace, even if you trip over a rock."

"Is that legal?"

"It may not be, but... You're in Mr. Bob's town. He makes the rules. The joke is that our town sheriff makes more money than the Governor."

"What does the county judge say about that?"

"What do you think? The judge is Mr. Bob's nephew—his sister's only boy."

"I see they do own this town."

"Town and county."

"Thanks for the warning. You really are a lucky charm. How far did you say this club is? Can I walk to it?"

"It's about two and a half miles from the city limit sign at the end of Main Street. Have fun."

5

New Friends

BARKLEY USUALLY CLOSED THE POST office at noon on Saturday so Jim decided a three-mile hike would be the thing to do He could taste the beer already. It dawned on him that he had not had a beer since coming to town. This town was starting to change him and maybe that wasn't all bad.

He must have been stepping lively because, before he knew it, he stood in front of the Supper Club. It was just as Sandy had described it. A one-story building that had many additions to it over the years, the building now in desperate need of paint. It was very apparent that the owner did not spend money on upkeep. He was sure that all the neon lights advertising different beer and wine must have been free because you could see no other signs of any advertising; not even the name of the band. When he thought about it, why did the club need to advertise? He was probably the only person for three counties that didn't know about the place.

He entered the door and immediately thought he hoped these folks were friendly. A bar fight was the last thing he was looking for under

his current agenda. He was relieved when a chubby old man behind the
bar yelled, "Welcome stranger! What's your poison?" By the look of his
big red nose it was obvious he liked to drink with his customers.

"Give me a beer."

"What kind?"

"Whatever you have on tap."

"You new around here?"

"Yes, only been in town a couple of weeks."

"Stayin' long?"

"Could be."

"Got a job yet?"

"Yeah, part time."

"You working at the mill?"

"No, working at the post office."

"You that kid that's been helpin' Mr. and Mrs. Barkley?"

"Well, I don't know about the kid part, but I am helping the
Barkleys, yes."

"Don't get your hackles up. When you are my age anyone younger
than 30 is a kid. Why didn't you say so? Your beer is on the house tonight!
It's all over town how you have put the sparkle in Mrs. Barkley's eyes and
brought back laughter to Mike. Seems you've brought 'em back from the
dead. Almost everybody in town thinks they hung the moon."

"You say almost everybody. Who doesn't?"

"That can wait until I know you a little better. Here's another beer.
It looks like that one had a hole in it."

"Looks a little dead around here. Am I wrong?"

"It's early. Wait a couple of hours and you can meet about everybody
from three counties."

"Any women?"

"Don't worry. They outnumber the guys two to one. Be careful
which gal you saddle up to, these old boys get a little jealous of strangers
tryin' to take their women, if you get my drift. Let me know which one
you have eyes for and I'll make the introduction for you. I owe you that
much for what you are doing for the Barkleys."

He ordered a hamburger and watched as the local folks began to arrive, mostly one at a time. As more and more people began to move in, the noise level rose. He moved over to the end stool at the bar. Someone put money into the jukebox and the music rose over the noise of the crowd, a few couples moving to the dance floor. As the music picked up in tempo and volume, the dance floor became almost too crowded. He watched the dancers and tapped his foot to the beat when a red haired, freckled-faced beauty approached him saying, "Does the rest of you move like your foot? If so, let's dance."

Remembering what the bartender had warned him about, Jim turned around and looked at him. It was hard to believe but he thought the bartender's nose was redder now than it had been two hours ago. The bartender saw him looking his way and just smiled and winked calling out, "Enjoy your dance."

After a couple of dances the beauty suggested they sit one out and have a cool one. He was so hypnotized by her green eyes that he would have agreed to walk on hot coals with bare feet just to gaze on her face for two minutes more. When they took two empty seats at the bar, the bartender sat two frosty mugs in front of them without asking.

"You're not from around here, are you?" she said to Jim, a coy look on her face.

"Now why would you say that?"

"Because you can actually keep up with me, dancing I mean."

"Is that so special?"

"I like to think so. All the guys around here want to get in my pants, dancing aside. Is that what you want?"

Jim had never met such an outspoken woman in all his twenty odd years. Despite the moment, he couldn't keep his face from a bright red flushed look. He tried to respond but all that would come out was, "Uh, uh, uh, no! I mean not right now."

She just laughed and as she did so, he was surprised that it bothered him so much. In fact he was thinking, I could fall in love with that laugh—and that wasn't a far stretch.

After he killed half his beer and recovered his speech, he asked, "Are you always this outspoken?"

"Only when I want to save time."

"Save time?"

"Yeah, if you didn't answer correctly I didn't want to waste the rest of the night."

"Did I answer correctly?"

"I'll let you know after a few more dances,"

No doubt about it. He was in love.

After several dances and as many beers, he had to find the men's room. As they walked off the dance floor, he told her he had to drain the main and headed straight to the restrooms. The break in the music caused a rush to the bathrooms and Jim quickly found out that his idea was not original. Being the new guy in the bar and unaware that during music breaks everyone had the same idea, he ended up at the end of the line.

Twenty minutes later, he returned to the bar and looked for his dance partner. After scanning every little cubbyhole he could see and without success, he went over to the bartender and asked, "Where did she go?"

"Who?"

"You know, the lady I was dancing with?"

"Oh, Peggy!"

"Is that her name?"

"She didn't tell you her name?"

"I didn't ask."

"Kid, you sure are slow. She left about ten minutes ago with her girlfriends."

"Who is she?"

"Well, I think I will let her tell you that if she wants to. I will tell you she is a school teacher in Jasper."

The weeks following he spent a great deal of time in the Club and got to know Nick, the bartender, quite well. At one time Nick had been the county sheriff in Fannin County. He had served long and well until one day he had an encounter with Mr. Bob Foster. Nick wouldn't tell him what the argument was about, just that in the fall election he only received sixteen votes. In the past, he had received every vote except for sixteen—

The job at the post office was uneventful and as reliable as day follows night... One day Jim was moving some big boxes in the back of the post office when Mr. Barkley came back and asked if he would like to eat lunch with them at the café down the street. Surprised, Jim just said, "I guess so. Yes, I do. Certainly!" When they walked into the café Mrs. Barkley took him around and introduced him to everyone there, including the cooks. He felt like a groom that was being introduced to his new family. The warm reception amazed him. It seemed the Barkleys really liked him. That being to the point, then everyone should.

As they ate lunch, without motivation or trying to stir up memories of the past, his mind went back to a time when he had Sunday dinner with his grandparents. Some of the only good times he could remember in his childhood and early adult years were with them.

The rest of the workday was post office-typical, and he felt warm and appreciated, a feeling he had never felt in his entire life. The Barkleys were real people, loving, forgiving and trustworthy.

In the next couple of weeks the Barkleys took him to lunch with them about twice a week. One day while eating in the café, Tastee Freeze Sandy came in for an ice cream. She waved and said hello. Mrs. Barkley whispered, "That's such a sad case."

Jim responded to her that he had heard her husband was hurt in the mill and couldn't work.

"That's true, but his getting hurt wasn't so bad at first because the mill provided them with a disability check. Her husband seemed to be adjusting to his injury and trying to make a new life for himself."

"What happened?"

"It's all that Foster boy's fault. He took a few law courses in Atlanta and came back just to advise his father. Apparently he found a loophole on paying disability to poor Ol' Bill and, I must say, other injured employees. With no more coverage, Bill lost his self-respect and desire to do anything. That Craig Foster is evil, big time Stay away from him,

Jim! When our Michael was in high school, he followed Craig Foster around like a little puppy. That Foster kid was abusive to Michael, down right low-life. I could not understand why Michael would always go back for more. They even went to the city to volunteer for the Army together. Can you believe it? Mr. Bob, who was then the head of the draft board here in Fannin County, warned them if they didn't volunteer he had to send them out with the next month's draftees. My Michael joined up the next week. When Craig came back to town a couple of months later he said they wouldn't take him!"

"Why?"

"We never found out. You read between the lines. Jim, stay away from evil!"

6

The Mission

THE NEXT COUPLE OF NIGHTS were tough getting to sleep. He kept thinking he was getting too involved with the Barkleys, the town, some of the nice people, that he should just complete the mission, collect the money and then take a well-deserved six months vacation in California, preferably Catalina. It had worked so well the three other times, why was he dragging his feet this time? He had cased the Tastee Freeze months ago and identified his target in the first few hours after he arrived. His plan had worked so well in the past. Why was he hesitating now? Could it be the Barkleys' kindness was having an effect on him, positive as it was? He knew they were trying to give him some of the love they had been unable to give their son, Michael. But he also had to admit that no one had ever gotten under his skin like Peggy. He didn't even know her last name. It had been almost a month since that night at the club, almost like a dream. Nick would not tell him anything about her. All he would say was that you didn't talk about a woman like her in a bar. Motivated primarily by pity, Nick finally revealed to him she usually came by the club at the end of each month. He made him promise on his life that he wasn't lying just to make him feel better. Nick laughed out loud.

"My God! You're in love and she might not even remember you."

"Don't say that, not even as a joke!"

This was the special weekend and he would know real soon if she were just a dream. If a dream, he could get on with his mission and collect his money without ever thinking about it again and thought California would be a good place to stay for the next six months.

It seemed noon would never arrive, especially on this day. As soon as Mr. Barkley directed him to lock the front door, he complied and then ran up the steps to take a quick shower and dress in the new clothes he had bought just to impress her. He assured himself she would be there. Living another day without seeing her would prove difficult. In his entire life, he had never felt this way about anyone. He didn't understand this strange new emotion and even stranger was the thought that he might not be able to control the parameters.

Walking a little faster, he stepped through the doors into the bar at exactly one thirty. Nick laughed, calling out, "Well, well—"

"Yeah, it's me—"

He slid a beer down the bar to him. "It's just you and me, kid. I guess you will have to wait a little longer." They both laughed.

About an hour later the silence was broken by someone coming through the bar doors. He could not believe his eyes. Talk about a bad dream! In the middle of the floor stood the worst imitation of the head guard you could ever imagine from his hats to his boots, ala *Cool Hand Luke* The glasses were perfect. He must have searched the whole state to find them. The only thing out of character was the pearl handle pistol on his side. The words just jumped out of his mouth, "What is that?"

"Are you looking for trouble, boy?"

He realized he had spoken too soon. "No, sir. I was just admiring your pearl handle pistol."

"Watch your tongue, son, and it's not pearl. It's modeled after General Patton's pistol. This is ivory. As Patton said, 'Only pimps carry pearl handled pistols' and I ain't no pimp.' "

Nick jumped in. "No, sir. This is Billy Bob Foster, the town sheriff for Blue Ridge, also the self-acclaimed best deer hunter in the state. The best gun collection, too. If you don't believe me, just ask him. Billy Bob, this is Jim Cole. He's new to our county."

"You got work?"

"Yes, sir. I work for Mr. Barkley at the post office."

"How long do you plan to stay?"

"Not sure. I thought I would have been gone by now but you really have a nice town here. I may stay until spring. Sir, can I look at your pistol?"

"Yeah, watch where you point it. It's loaded and I carry it with the safety off."

Nick looked at him and thought, *What a moron!* "Billy Bob, that's going to get you killed one day."

"You're not sheriff anymore so pipe down. Now days we need to get our weapons out quickly. You never know what dope head you might run into."

"Or a revenging wife."

"You weren't there. Self-defense all the way."

"Yeah, those one hundred and fifty-pound women sure can scare a man! How many shots did it take? Three? No, no, four. All in the chest, right? Billy Bob is our town woman killer."

"That's enough, now." Billy Bob gave Nick a stare that said if he could get away with it he would kill him right on the spot.

"What are you going to do? Tell your Uncle Bob and have me fired? If you do, who will serve you free beer?"

Trying to cool things down, Jim said, "Sheriff, is the deer hunting good around here?"

Billy Bob relaxed a bit and said, "Not as good as it is in South Georgia, but we find plenty. Do you hunt?"

"I did a couple of times with my father when I was a teenager. We never saw a deer. I think the deer were smarter than we were."

"They are not smart. They just have good ears and noses," Billy Bob said. "If you'd like, I can give you some pointers."

"I'd like that, but I don't have a gun."

"What kind of gun are you looking for?"

"My dad had an old Army rifle he converted to a hunting rifle. I'm not sure what kind it was. He just called it his 03. I loved shooting it. Do you know what kind of gun that was?"

"That's easy. Before WW1 the Army used the Springfield 03. Springfield Arms made them and 1903 was the first year the Army began to use them. I must have at least five in my closet. They need to be modified, but I know a guy in Atlanta that can do that for you. He might be able to complete it in time for deer season."

"How much will it cost me?"

"Well, I got a real deal on the weapon. How about $20 for the gun? I can get Kurt to modify it for you for another $30. Can you afford $50 for the best deer gun ever?"

"Oh, yes. I can do that. What else do I need?"

"If you want to see deer, you need to make sure they don't smell you. You'll need a pair of knee-high boots and gloves."

"Rubber boots?"

"Yeah, come outside and I'll show you mine. I keep them in the trunk of my car."

As Billy Bob opened the trunk, Jim asked what size boot he wore.

"Eleven. What size do you need?"

"Nine and a half, maybe ten."

"You will need to make sure they fit or you will end up with blisters."

"I understand that. Where can I get a pair like yours?"

"I got them at Johnson's Bait and Tackle Shop on South Main Street. I think they were $9.95. Are you interested in that gun?"

"Oh, yes."

"How about the gunsmith?"

"I don't have a car. I don't know how I can get the gun to him."

"That's easy. I go see him every other Thursday. Do you want to ride with me this Thursday?"

"I would love to. I'll see if Mr. Barkley will let me off that day. I'd be grateful for the ride. Billy Bob, why are you going so far out of your way to help me?"

"Currently I've run out of hunting buddies and it's always more fun to hunt with someone."

"Well, it looks like you found a new hunting buddy. Thanks for the help."

"Well, I've got to go make my rounds. See you later, Jim. It was Jim, wasn't it?"

"Yes, Jim Cole. I'll let you know what Mr. Barkley says about the day off."

As Jim came back into the bar, Nick called out, "Did Billy Bob convince you he was the greatest hunter since Daniel Boone?"

"Not really. He did say he had run out of hunting buddies. How come?"

"Remember, he was not using the safety on his pistol? Yeah, well, that's the way he hunts, too. Nobody in this county wants to be in the same woods with him. Billy Bob has been known to shoot at sounds. It wouldn't surprise anyone if he blew his own head off one day. If I were you, I'd stay out of the woods when he's there."

"Sounds like good advice. I'll remember that."

7
A Lady

AFTER A COUPLE OF HOURS drinking, the beer that Nick kept fresh was starting to have an effect on him. The thought of being drunk when he might see Peggy terrified him.

"Stop the beer, already! Gimme a Coke and I need to eat— Two burgers and fries? Thought you were my friend! Why are you trying to get me drunk?"

"If she doesn't show I could just throw you out with the trash."

He looked at his watch for the hundredth time, 9:21 p.m., one minute later than last time—

Just as he thought he could not stand it any longer, there she was. He would have staked his life there was a special light shining only on her, every time she smiled, every time she moved. She was here and for the life of him he didn't know what to do. Nick looked at him and just smiled. She worked her way up to the bar. "Peggy, would you put this kid out of his misery. He thinks you actually remember him, but he's afraid to ask."

All Jim could do was give a sheepish grin.

"I didn't at first, but I do remember that red face and grin. Jim Cole, are you ready to dance the night away?"

"Yes, ma'am. And you remembered my name. A bit more than just 'red face and grin.' Don't you think?"

"Wait a minute— How do you know my name?"

"Us country folks have our ways."

He enjoyed himself that night like he never knew possible. When a slow song was played and he could hold her in his arms, his whole body trembled. He kept thinking if any two bodies fit together in this world, theirs did. Something strange was happening. It was as if they had known each other all their lives. She was his angel and he wondered if she knew...

All at once he was afraid of what to do next. *What am I going to do?* he thought. *She's used to men falling for her then telling them to drop dead. Now, Jim, just keep calm. What would James Bond do? That's it! He'd knock her off balance. How do I do that?* While he was thinking, the answer was there in front of his face. One of her friends came over and asked her to the restroom. Without ado, she just walked off with her friend leaving him standing there. *That's it!* he thought. She left without a word last time when I was in the restroom. Turnabout's fair play.

He walked up to Nick to tell him good night.

"Where's Peggy?"

"In the little girl's room with her friend."

"So you are leaving her like she did you?"

"Yeah, something like that."

"Great move, kid. I may have underestimated you. See you next week. Hurry up...get outta here— Hey, anything you want me to tell her—if she asks, that is?"

"If she asks...tell her you think I'll be here next Saturday. Got it?"

"Great answer, kid. You're good!"

8

Michael & Susan

BEING ALONE ON SUNDAYS MADE the day seem forty-eight hours long. It was amazing how accustomed he had become to a solid comfort level with the Barkleys. Time just seemed to fly when they were around. Of course, the time flying with them was no comparison to time spent with Peggy. He had awoke at 5:30 a.m. and, predictably, couldn't go back to sleep. It was now 8:00 a.m. and felt like noon. What was he going to do until tomorrow, when he could talk to Nick?

He stood up and looked about the room. Mr. Barkley had given him permission to move things around and if he wanted to remove anything to just put it in the shed outside. One chair had to go. *Now where did I put the key? Oh, yeah, on the nail next to the door.* He thought he should check out the shed before he carried the heavy chair down the steep stairs.

The key fit. However, the lock acted like it hadn't been opened in years, stiff, rusty and laden with dirt. He walked upstairs and retrieved a little WD-40 spray lubricant and shot a couple of squirts on every place he thought might help make the lock work better. After some seconds, the lock snapped open. Placing more oil on the lock, he exercised it until it worked as good as new. This little job completed made him feel like a new man.

Jim then had a look inside the shed. He opened the double doors wide and stepped in. It was like a time capsule. It appeared as if the user of the shed had just closed the door one day expecting to use the tools the next day; however, the next day never arrived. On the left wall, neatly hung, were garden tools. That seemed strange to him because he could see no signs of a garden outside. He looked out the open door thinking he might have overlooked something. The yard was behind the post office and surrounded by buildings on all sides. At the back of the yard was an old pathway. The yard looked as if it were a product of weeds growing to maturity and then falling over to be replaced with a new crop of weeds the next year. At one time there might have been a garden, though no sign of it remained.

He returned his interest to the shed. The only thing out of place was an old green duffle bag lying on a bench. This bag must be the belongings of Michael that the Army had sent to the Barkleys. He put out his hand to touch the bag and before he could touch it he jerked his hand back like it had touched a fire. A strange sense of reverence came over him. He had the same feelings as he had the first time he visited the graves of his mother and sister. The emotions brought back the anger that had been driving him for the last eight years. He looked at the bag—all that was left of an American hero—one green bag. Shameful. *Where's the justice in that?* he thought. People like Mr. Bob and his son spend their whole lives taking advantage of everyone around them, making sure if they find someone down and out they supply an additional kick. What is their punishment? Parks, roads and buildings named in their honor—

He sat down on an old bar stool and just looked at what was left of the Barkley's son. The reflection of the sun off a mirror broke the trance. He quickly looked at his watch. It was 2:00 p.m. He had been thinking, reminiscing and just plain sitting around for almost two hours. Then he remembered why he was in the shed in the first place. He saw where he could put Michael's bag and have it out of the way.

In the right corner was a nail, or more like a spike. It would be more than adequate to hold the weight. He picked up the bag and turned it around to find the latch at the top. It would be just the thing to slide over the nail. When he turned it around, he saw a very disturbing sight. The end of the bag had been up against the wall and a family of rats had made themselves at home. All that was left at the top was the latch. It looked strange with the latch securely locked with a military padlock but the latch and lock were no longer attached to the bag.

He opened the top of the bag and looked inside. Some of the contents looked damaged. What should he do? It might be too painful for Mr. and Mrs. Barkley right now. When they talked about Michael now, they seemed to have happy memories. Would looking at his things in this bag bring bad ones to the surface? Now a good idea.

He decided he would look through it and take out anything he thought might upset the Barkleys. He would repack it and then tell them about the rats making a hole in the top of the bag. They might not even want to look at the contents. He picked up the bag and turned it upside down and let the contents fall out. Four field rats made their escape to the weeds outside. *What a brave man you are, Jim Coleman! COLE, you fool! You cannot afford to make that mistake again,* he thought.

The bag appeared to have been packed by a military man. Socks, shorts, and t-shirts were rolled. Khaki shirts and pants were neatly folded. Two Khaki uniforms, five sets of socks, shorts and t-shirts, a shaving kit, a pair of shoes and one pair of boots. Two pairs of blue jeans and two short-sleeve civilian shirts were the only non-military items. Not much, but apparently all this soldier seemed to need. Under the civilian shirts, Jim found a small wooden box. When he opened it, he found badges, pins, rank insignia, tie, pen, a small rock and a pack of letters from someone by the name of Susan.

On top was a letter addressed to Susan Barkley, Blue Ridge, Georgia. The letter was not sealed. This must have been the last letter Michael had written. He opened it and began to read...

Dear Susan,

I received three letters from you today. Don't be concerned, I looked at the date at the top of each letter to make sure I read them in order. Honey, you can't ever know how much I miss you. I just wish I could hold you in my arms and smell your hair. I better stop this or I'll need a cold shower! Like we have hot showers! Ha Ha.

Sweetie, I'm so glad you took the chaplain's advice and saw the doctor in Atlanta. Chaplain Kuhlbars told me that we have such a special relationship. He said he has seen more "Dear John" letters than he could count and it was nice to see a couple that were truly in love. He said most wives would never have shared with their husbands what happened to you. He thinks because there are no secrets between us that there is nothing we cannot accomplish.

Speaking of accomplishments, my platoon leader, Capt. Sam Wright, is from Atlanta. He plans to return to his job as a GA State Trooper. I have discussed Mr. Bob and Craig with him. Capt. Wright vowed they are only big fish in a very, very small pond. I told him I wanted to settle some score with them when I get home. I assured him I wanted to do it legal and all. He has promised me all the help I need. Don't worry. I didn't tell him what they did to you. Susan, I promise I will settle the score with them..

Major Patterson called CW2 Larson and me into his office this afternoon. I thought we were in trouble at first. The major just smiled and told us to sit down short timers. When you get close to going home, that's what they call you (Short). I told him I was so short I could sit on a nickel and use a dime for a footstool. He laughed and asked me how many days I had. I told him 18 and wakeup. Larson has 22 and a wakeup. He then said he had good news for us. They need a helicopter at Fire Base Nancy for the next three weeks. All we need to do each day is fly to Nancy, land and wait to fly the commander when he needs us. He laughed saying we might get 6 more hours of flying here in Nam. He hoped we would enjoy them.

Sweetie, it's getting really late. I'll close now and mail it tomorrow when I get back from Nancy. Then I will only have 17 and a wakeup. Hey, I love you.

Your Michael Mouse

He couldn't believe it. He'd had only 17 days left to serve. He had so much left to do. *Well, Michael, tell you what... Maybe I can help you settle that score,* Jim thought. He repacked the bag as neatly as he could and placed the box in the middle of the bag with Michael's civilian clothes on top. Luckily the rats had destroyed only one of the civilian shirts when creating their nest. He placed the shirt in the bag last. When he finished he looked with a little pride on how well he had repacked the bag. It looked as if it was packed years ago and with the exception of the rats, had never been touched. He placed the bag on a box in the corner. He planned to find the right time Monday morning to approach Mr. Barkley about the damage from the rats and ask what he thought should be done. He could see how the personal letters could cause a great deal of heartache; therefore, he placed them inside his shirt. He would read the letters and hopefully clear up the mystery of why she needed to see a doctor in Atlanta. He was also very curious as to why the chaplain thought they had such a special relationship. He had never had a close relationship with anyone in his entire life, so he was very skeptical that one could exist in the real world. Oh, he had read about such relationships in books and seen them in movies, but everyone knew that wasn't the way life was, not any day of the week.

He took the letters upstairs and placed them under a loose board he had discovered while moving his bed. He picked up the chair that he had planned to move six hours before and, exhausted, he placed it in the corner of the shed. Funny, the chair looked horrible in his apartment but so comfortable in the shed. Why was that? He just had to see if it was in fact comfortable and chose his moment to sit down. He was surprised to find that it was. If he only had a little table he would be all set. Then he remembered the table in his bathroom that was just in the way (the table that had given him more than one bruise as he stepped out of the shower) he thought this might work. As he was climbing the steps to get the table, he decided it was time to find a pen and paper to start a list of things he would need for the coming mission. Of all his missions, this one seemed the most justified.

9
The Plan

SEVERAL MINUTES LATER HE HAD the table in the shed with paper and pen, ready to start planning. He thought, *Where do I start? Maybe instead of trying to put everything in order, I'll just list the things I already know I need.* He began to write.

1. A pair of knee-high rubber boots, size 11 (Get at Johnson's Bait & Tackle)
2. A compass
3. 30-06 rifle with scope
4. Map of the area
5. Mr. Bob's phone number
6. As much info possible on Mr. Bob & Craig
7. Scout out the access to Mr. Bob's house
8. How to take time off without arousing the Barkley's suspicions

As he put the paper aside, a detailed plan began to form in his mind. He smiled to himself and mused, *I think I have found my calling.* He cautioned himself to not forget his number one rule—don't fool yourself. Plan, plan and plan again and then follow the plan. This small, southern town needs you.

When he saw Mrs. Barkley leave and go towards the café the next morning, he realized it was the perfect time to talk with Mr. Barkley. He walked up to his desk at the front of the post office and asked, "Sir, can I have a moment of your time?"

"Of course you can, son. What's on your mind?"

"A couple of things. First, when I came here a couple months ago I didn't think I would be staying so long."

"Are you planning to leave?"

"No! It's not that. It's just that I have a close friend from my hometown who has a job that requires him to travel a lot. We made plans to meet in Atlanta next Thursday at the Red Lobster on Peachtree. He's buying the beer and lobster this time. Would it be okay if I take that day off?"

"What a relief! I thought we were losing you. Do you want me to drive you to the city?"

"No, sir. I'll just take the morning bus and return on the first bus I can."

"Great. Go and have a good time with your friend," Mr. Barkley said. "Friends are the only things worth having."

Jim got a little uncomfortable, primarily because he was deceiving the best friend he had ever had, so he quickly changed the subject to not dwell on feeling bad about himself.

"Sir, I finally moved that big chair down to the shed yesterday."

"That's good. The missus and I want you to make yourself at home."

"Thanks. I noticed a lot of garden tools in the shed. Whose tools are they and where is the garden?"

"Those were Michael's tools. He loved to see things grow, especially tomatoes. He also raised cucumbers, carrots, lettuce and radishes. I used to kid him that those were the most expensive vegetables in the county. He would look at me, and say, 'But aren't they the best tasting ones in the world?' Those were wonderful times, watching things grow and all."

"I'm sorry I brought back bad memories."

"Oh, NO, son. Those were the best days of my life. Thanks for reminding me."

"Would you mind me cleaning up the back yard and maybe we could plant some tomatoes next spring?"

"What a great idea. You should have all the tools you need in the shed."

"One last thing, while I was in the shed I moved Michael's duffle bag."

"Don't worry, we should have taken it home a long time ago."

"It's not that, sir. When I moved it, I noticed a family of rats had set up their home in one end of the bag. It looked like the only damage was to that one end. I just wondered what you want me to do. I didn't want to tell you in front of Mrs. Barkley."

"Thanks. I'm not sure how she would respond to such news. If you will loan me the key, I will check it out later and decide if she even needs to know."

"Is this the only key?"

"Yes, we lost the other one years ago, but you're the only one who needs one anyway."

As he and Mr. Barkley walked back to the front of the post office a customer called out, "Mike, I have a package that was too big for my box. Could you get it for me?"

"Well, well, if it isn't Jerry Huff. How are you, you old crook?"

"Oh, I'm doing fine, how about you?"

"Fine, fine. Getting ready for deer season?"

"Not really, you know there are just not that many deer up here in these mountains. Squirrel season opened the September 15. Got my limit Saturday. In fact, Helen and I had gravy and biscuits with squirrel for breakfast."

"Boy, does that sound good. You know Mother stopped cooking a few years back."

While Mr. Barkley and the customer talked he saw his chance. He moved to the desk. An old, well-used phone book was under the phone. He quickly turned to the section he needed. Finding a scrap of paper and he wrote down the City Hall's number. He then turned the pages looking for Bob Foster's number. Just as he thought—not listed. As he was putting the phone book back, Mr. Barkley, smiling, commented, "You found a friend you might want to call?"

"No, sir. No such luck. I was just wondering if the town had any Cole's in it."

"You should have just asked me. I know everybody in Blue Ridge, Route 1 and 2. The only Cole I can think of lives in McCaysville."

"Where is that?"

"A small town eleven miles north on Highway 5. It's located on the Georgia/Tennessee line. On the Georgia side is McCaysville and on the Tennessee side is Copperhill. It's none of my business, but I would steer clear of there if I were you. It's like all border towns, the only thing you'll find there is trouble."

"Thanks, I'll remember that. I'm going to the drug store to get a Coke. Can I get something for you?"

"Why, yes, that would be nice. Get me a large black coffee. Tell them it's for me."

"I will, sir."

As he entered the drug store, he could see it was empty. He walked up to the counter and requested a large Coke and a large black coffee to go. "By the way," he said, "Mr. Barkley, told me to tell you the coffee was for him." The lady laughed and said she would take care of it.

Jim looked around and asked if they had a pay phone. She pointed it out near the front door. He made his way to the phone, read the instructions and dialed the number he had written down at the post office. A lady answered, "City Hall. Can I help you?"

"I'd like to speak to Billy Bob."

"Who's calling and can I give him a subject?"

"It's Jim and the subject is hunting."

"I'll put you right through."

When Billy Bob answered, he identified himself and told him he was free to ride to Atlanta on Thursday if it was still okay.

"Okay? You've made my week. Did you tell Mr. Barkley you were going with me?"

"No, sir. Mr. Barkley doesn't like you very much."

"What an understatement!"

"If it's okay, I will just meet you in front of City Hall."

"That's a good plan," Billy Bob said, deadpan. "Be there around 7:30 a.m. and just come on inside. I will have just completed my rounds and we can have coffee before we leave."

"Billy Bob, thanks so much. I will be there Thursday morning."

10

Big Red Foster

JIM WALKED BACK TO THE counter and placed his money on top of the bill. "Can you tell me what's so special about this coffee?" he asked.

The waitress laughed and said, "Mr. Barkley is like a lot of the old timers around here. They grew up during the depression. The coffee they could get was more chicory than coffee, but they developed a taste for it. Also, the way they made coffee back then, there were always grounds in the bottom of the cup. I'm not sure I should share my secret with you because everybody over sixty comes here for the coffee."

"Ma'am, I've just got to know. I'm working for the Barkleys, and I will do anything to make them happy. I'm so sorry I didn't introduce myself. My name is Jim."

"Hi, I'm Judy. If you promise never to repeat it, I'll tell you."

"I promise."

"I put in a half teaspoon of freshly ground coffee beans. That gives the coffee the bite in taste they are looking for and the grounds in the bottom of the cup."

"Your secret is safe with me. I'll see you later."

As he walked up to the front door he could see Mrs. Barkley had returned. When Mr. Barkley came to open the door for him, he handed him his coffee.

"Is that a park or something across the street?"

They walked to the corner of the building across the street, a large white house located at the center and back of the lot. The lot had well-manicured grass with not one tree. The street across from the post office had six concrete steps climbing to a 5-foot wide walkway that ran up the middle of the lot to the front steps of the house. The walk was more than one hundred feet in length. The yard sloped downward from the walk and met the side walkway. It appeared that when it was built, the house was probably the largest in town, if not in the county. It had been designed with a great deal of pride and looked like a castle that had been deserted by its knight.

Mr. Barkley looked as if he was thinking back to his childhood. "Big Red Foster built that house before I was born. He is the granddaddy of all the Fosters in the county and he was well liked by everyone who knew him. Big Red started the empire. At one time he had lumber supply yards in every town for fifty miles in any direction. The lumber supply he started here is located on the north part of town next to the ball field. When we were kids, Big Red would have picnics and games on the front lawn, as he called it. This would go on all summer long. He liked being around people. He even built a large public pool for all the kids to swim in during the summer. Blue Ridge was a great place for kids to grow up. They had to close all the pools down in the county back in the 1940s when we had an outbreak of polio. Public pools never came back, never did. People began to spend time on Lake Blue Ridge. You wouldn't believe it, but Big Red knew everybody that worked for him by his first name. At one time the number must have been over two thousand people. He was the most humble and honorable man I have every known."

"If Big Red was so respected, what happened with Mr. Bob?"

"That was the problem. Everyone that knew his father liked him, respected him and looked up to him as the leader of the community. When he passed on, Mr. Bob wanted the same status as his father. A better statement is that he demanded the same respect as his father. Son, respect is something you must earn, not demand. Mr. Bob never learned this lesson. In fact, the more he demanded it, the more the people lost respect for Little Bobby. Little Bobby was a nickname the people gave him. When he would hear them call him that he would go into a blind rage. He put out an order to everyone that worked for him that they would address him as Mr. Bob. This order was to apply to the employee's family as well."

"Didn't the people object?"

"Oh, a couple of young men refused to call him that."

"What happened?"

"He fired both of them on the spot. Most of the older employees complied with little complaints. However, the younger men did not like being talked down to, or sideways for that matter. The people around here have a lot of pride and do not like to be walked on. One of the young employees said something that day that has proven to be true."

"What was that?"

"As the young man left the work area, he looked at Mr. Bob and said, 'Little Bobby, you don't realize we don't need you. YOU need us.' "

"What did Mr. Bob do?"

"He went into another blind rage and looking around he fired anyone that laughed or even smiled. The downfall of the lumber mill began right then and there."

"What a tragic end to a great man's legacy."

"That's true, son, but believe it or not it gets worse. During the depression and the great World War Two, times were hard on the merchants around here, like real hard. Mr. Bob was quick to loan them money of course, as much as they needed. At the time, many thought him a Godsend. It seemed he had truly changed and was becoming a community leader like his father. Then the truth really came out—the real Mr. Bob popped up his ugly head."

"And...?"

"In the loan papers that he required the merchants to sign was a clause stating if they missed as few as one payment he would become the majority owner of their businesses—mind you, just one delinquent payment."

"It's hard to believe the businessmen would have overlooked such a clause! All it would take is one person to see what was really going on and the word would have spread like wildfire."

"Yes, true enough, but they were so desperate for cash they would have signed their wives away."

Mr. Barkley took a long drink from his coffee and said, "Judy Adams made this coffee."

"How did you know?"

"Because she makes the best coffee in town. It has bite. Thanks."

"You're welcome, sir." Embarrassed to have brought up such a touchy subject, he turned back to Mr. Bob's yard and asked, "Do they have picnics now?"

"No way! In fact if you walk on one blade of grass, Mr. Bob will set his dog, Butch, on you."

"Butch?"

"Oh, yeah... Indeed, he went to Atlanta looking for the meanest dog he could find."

"Does he hate people that much?"

"Not people. Kids mostly..."

"Kids?"

"Yes. The elementary school is located on the hill right above his house. Come to think of it, the only thing he wasn't able to move, eradicate or otherwise manipulate. The kids loved to walk on the grass and take shortcuts across his lawn to get home. After all, why not, right? Mr. Bob used to shout at them but the kids eventually ignored his threats—until he found Butch, of course. He brags that Butch has bitten over twenty kids and scared more than a hundred."

"Doesn't anyone complain to the police?"

"Why, what good would it do? He owns the city sheriff and the judge. If the thing ever got to court, it would be thrown out anyway."

"No one should be able to control other people's lives like that, no one."

"That's funny. That's exactly what Michael wrote in his last letter to us.

"Mr. Barkley, trust me, maybe that will change some day."

"I hope so. Jim, it's about time you started calling me Mike. What do you think? You calling me Mr. all the time makes me feel old."

"Thank you Mr.—I mean, Mike, I would like that. What should I call Mrs. Barkley?"

"She would love for you to call her Mother Barkley, all the youngsters around here do. After a while, if you would like to just call her Mother. Would put a sparkle in her eyes. She would love it."

"Thanks, Mike."

11
Woman Killer

"It's going home time." The words that just might change his life. Now he would find out if Peggy had asked about him. It was silly, he was sure. He was acting like a schoolboy who kept asking his friends if the prettiest girl in school liked him. Peggy must have been the prettiest girl in her school, Jim was sure. It's amazing how quickly three miles can pass on foot when you're in a hurry.

As he walked into the bar, he saw Nick pouring a beer.

"Hey, the lovesick puppy, isn't it?"

"Come on. Gimme a break."

"Relax, kid. How have you been?"

"Great, I guess. The more I learn about this town the more amazed I am that anyone stays."

"Hey, well put, ol' friend. It's a mystery to me, too. So what did you learn today?"

"Mike gave me the history of Big Red and Mr. Bob."

"So it's Mike now, huh?"

"Yes, he wants me to call him Mike. I'm still not comfortable with it, but what the hay."

"You'll get there. Did Mike also tell you about Butch?"

"Oh, yeah, that information was the focal point of the story. The kid chaser."

"Did he also tell you that Mr. Bob loves that dog more than life itself?"

"No, he didn't say anything about that."

"Well, Butch may be the meanest dog in the world to everyone else but he loves Mr. Bob with an unconditional love of a sled dog. Come to think of it, only Butch loves Mr. Bob. Not even his children really care for him."

"In a sense, that's a shame," Jim said.

"Well, he earned all ten yards of it. You must love to be loved, you know. Speaking of love, Peggy asked about you."

"She did? What did she say?" Jim said.

"She wanted to know where her dancing partner went. I told her you left with a blonde."

"You didn't!"

"No, just kidding. I told her you had to leave but you would be back Saturday night."

"What did she say?"

"Nothing."

"Nothing?" Jim wondered.

"Just smiled and joined her friends."

"Do you think she will be here Saturday?"

"Do bears live in the woods?"

"What?"

"Kid, you worry too much. Just be here on Saturday."

Jim ordered another beer. While pondering the meaning of life on the bar stool, he realized for the first time in his life, for the very first time, he was comfortable talking to a friend. Nick was never judgmental and seemed to understand how he felt about things. Bartenders were like that but Nick was special, even for a bartender. *I'll miss Nick when I finish my mission,* he thought. *If only...*

"Was Michael Barkley married?"

"Kid, I thought you knew."

"No, the Barkleys mention him off and on but I don't push it. I wouldn't want to upset them."

"Yes, he was. He and Susan Wilson married in Hawaii while Michael was on leave from the service."

"Where is she now?"

"Not sure you want to know."

"Why?

"What was it you said when you came in? The more you learn the more you wonder why people stay here?"

"What has that got to do with Susan?"

"Remember when I told you Billy Bob was a woman killer?"

"Yeah—"

"Well, the woman he killed was Susan."

"What?"

"Shortly after she was notified of Michael's death, Billy Bob went for a visit. As he explained it, she just went crazy and he shot her in self-defense."

"What did the investigation say?"

"What investigation? Billy Bob just made a report and the judge conducted a closed inquest."

Here it was, right between the eyes. Now Jim was blazing mad. This news really disturbed him to the core. He wished Nick good night and slowly walked home. He wondered why so many good people had looked the other way as a few evil people took over their community. Would they know what to do if asked to stand up for themselves?

It was another sleepless night.

The next day found Mike in an unusually talkative mood. He didn't have anything really to say, but when ending a story laughed out loud to such an extent that people outside could hear him. His laugh was infectious, too. He now began to notice the small group of people always hanging around the post office. Mike had even put a bench out front so they could sit. He understood why, Mike was a wonderful person to be around.

The evening found him eating a couple of sandwiches in his room. When he finished the quick meal he opened the loose boards under his bed and removed Michael's letters. Maybe the letters could answer some of the questions he had come up with over the past few days. As he looked at the small stack of letters, one envelope looked more worn than the others. He decided to read this one first—

My dearest Michael,

I know it has been a long time since my last letter. This is the hardest thing I have ever had to do. I have something to tell you. Something happened and I just didn't know what to do. I thought about waiting until you got home because you are so far away and I know how crazy this is going to make you. I don't want you to do something that will get you hurt. Then I realized that not telling you would be the same as lying if I deliberately kept something from you. So here goes. Michael, know that I love you with all my heart. What I have to tell you is going to hurt you terribly and if you decide you no longer want me as your wife, I truly will understand.

Just after I got back from Hawaii I moved to Thelma and Frank's cabin on the lake. Leaving you and knowing you were heading into harm's way was so hard. I needed some time to myself, so Thelma suggested I move there.

Everything was great for a couple of weeks. Everyone left me alone. Then Craig stopped by to see me one night saying you'd kill him if he didn't check on me once in a while. I thought it was real nice of him. We had coffee and talked about you, high school and just stuff.

Two nights later he came back and he was drunk. I told him he couldn't come in like that and it enraged him. He shoved his way in and grabbed me, hitting me in the face. I tried to stop him, I really did, but he was all over me and was way too strong. He threw me on the floor and raped me. Afterwards I was fighting him and crying and trying to cover myself and he just stood there laughing at me calling me horrible names. He said I was his whore now. I stayed in for days crying, not knowing what to do or whether I should tell anyone. Who could I tell? Two weeks later he came back. I wouldn't go to the door and it made him so mad he kicked in the back door and just went crazy. He kicked my feet out from under me and then just started kicking and hitting me all over before he raped me again. I was hysterical and he kept laughing like a crazy person and telling me if I didn't cooperate with him when he came he'd tell everyone I was whoring for him. I just kept screaming for him to get out. I was hurt really bad this time Michael. The next morning I was so messed up I couldn't let anyone see me. I decided I'd stay there until I looked good enough to go to Mom's without her asking questions. Every night I lived in fear. I sat on the edge of the porch closest to the bushes and when I heard the gravel as he turned in the road. I 'd run into the woods and hide until he gave up and left. I did this night after night until my face got better. As soon as I could, I packed up and left.

Michael, this is the worst part. I have some kind of infection. It's really bad. When I called Craig to ask what he had given me he said, "You stupid tramp. You have the clap." Then he laughed and hung up. I just don't know what to do. I can't tell my parents and telling Billy Bob would be lunacy. I truly have nowhere to go for help. I tried to stop him. I swear to you I did. I hope that you can find it in your heart to forgive me, but if you can't I accept your decision. But as my best friend on this earth, please tell me what to do.

He stopped reading and sat very still for the longest time. *To think I only came here to take petty revenge on another bully and his son and now I have discovered a major travesty in justice that needs righting, all coming together in one fell swoop*, he thought. *Ain't life great—*

He picked up the letter and held it tight. *Michael, Susan, you will get your revenge*, he vowed. *Trust me on that one, you will, I promise.* After getting up off the floor he walked to the kitchen to find some matches.

He quickly found a small box. Down the back stairs to the garden he went. After digging a hole about two feet across and six inches deep, he placed all the letters into the hole. He knew instinctively that burning the letters was the right thing to do. These letters would kill the Barkleys. *Too many good people have suffered in this town,* he thought while gritting his teeth. *It's time the evil ones felt the pain.*

The next morning he looked at the Barkleys in a new light of compassion, all the while thinking he was glad they were not aware of how their son and his wife had been so violated.

12

The Hunter

SINCE THE DAY HE DRANK Judy's first cup of coffee it had become a pleasant routine. Walking back to the post office with the afternoon refreshment, he decided to observe the children going by Mr. Bob's place on their way home from school. He placed one of the chairs Mike had provided for the growing crowd near the corner of the post office and sat drinking his Coke while watching the kids playing down the sidewalk. Without warning, a large, black dog began chasing them, children running in all directions. One of the smaller children fell and the dog grabbed him and shook the child like a rag doll. Just as he thought the kid was dead, a whistle blew and the dog dropped the child and ran to his master.

Jim was sick to his stomach. A crowd joined the small child and then someone arrived with a car and took the injured child away. He decided some long-range revenge would be the order of the day, and real soon.

That night Jim opened his large suitcase and took out a long, wooden box. Using a large screwdriver he removed the top board. Inside was a state-of-the-art riflescope. It was the only item he had taken along from previous missions. He took the scope from its case and wrapped it in a kitchen towel. He placed the scope and towel into a large paper bag. He then wrote three quick letters, addressed them and placed a stamp on each. After placing them in the bag with the scope he knew he was ready.

Just as he rounded the corner next to the bus station Billy Bob pulled his police car in front of the city jail. As Billy Bob exited the car he saw him. "Early bird," Billy Bob said.

"Guess so."

"That's great. Come on in. Let's have a cup of coffee."

Jim walked into the office and was shocked at what he saw.

"Looks like you are going to war. Never saw so many maps in all my life."

"A lot of maps of the same area, that's all."

"What do you mean?" Jim said.

"Each year I plot the deer sign I find. The next year I transfer all the old plots to a new map. With all this information I'm able to pattern the bucks in the area. Deer, like people, are creatures of habit. They seem to travel the same trail each year."

"What kind of sign do you plot?"

"Deer rubs and scrapes."

"What's a scrape?"

"Oh, that's how the buck lets the doe in the area know he's around. The buck will scrape the ground clean of leaves and sticks with his front feet. He'll then urinate in the middle. When a doe comes by, she'll smell him. If she's ready to breed, she will wait around for the buck that made the scrape. A rub is where a buck will rub all the bark off a small tree. He does this first to get the velvet off his antlers, but later he's just marking his territory."

"You sure know a lot about deer."

"The more you know the better the chance you'll be successful."

"I can see that," Jim said with a smile. "Where can I get a copy of those maps?"

"Here. I have a couple extras. Take these."

"Oh, I couldn't—" Jim feinted.

"Yeah, you could. You need to know the area we'll hunt."

"Where will that be?"

Billy Bob took the map he had given him and drew a small circle on the bottom of the left-hand side of the sheet. "Take it home with you and study it."

"I will, thanks."

"Are you ready to get on the road?"

"You bet."

They had not been on the road for more than ten minutes when Billy Bob exclaimed, "Oh, my God! I forgot to let Mr. Bob know I'm gone for the day."

"Do we need to go back?" Jim said.

"No, there's a service station just down the road. I'll use their pay phone."

Billy Bob pulled hard into the gas station parking area, hopped out with the engine running and made his call. Only then did he seem to relax. He walked back to the car to let Jim know he was going in to get a cup of coffee and to see if he wanted one.

"Yeah, thanks, make mine black."

As soon as Billy Bob walked away and into the convenience store, he went to the pay phone and quickly dialed the operator. She came on the line with, "Number, please."

"Ma'am, I'm working with Billy Bob. Some kids have been making prank bomb calls to the principal of the school. We are trying to find which phone they used. Another prank call was made a few minutes ago. Could you please give me the last number called from this phone?"

"My name's Stacy. You tell Billy Bob this gives me a freebee. Okay?"

"I will."

"The number is 632-7676."

He thanked her for the help and walked back to the car. Billy Bob came out with the coffee just as Jim settled back down in the car seat. Figuring that Jim just used the phone, he asked, "Called your girl?"

"No, I remembered I left my hot plate turned on. Called Mr. Barkley so he could turn it off for me."

"It wouldn't do for you to burn down the post office, would it!"

As they traveled to Atlanta, Billy Bob became more talkative. Jim discovered if he sounded impressed by what he was saying the stories got even bigger and more exaggerated.

"Billy Bob, how long have you been Blue Ridge Sheriff?"

"Mr. Bob had the mayor appoint me the summer I got out of high school."

"Wow, right out of high school?" Jim said.

"Yeah, he wanted someone to control the kids taking short cuts across his yard. He fixed that problem a couple of years ago."

He avoided asking the follow up question and instead said, "You seem to like your job."

"Well, why not? When I was in high school I couldn't even get a date. Now I get more pussy than anyone in town, except maybe Craig."

"The girls around here like uniforms that much?"

"No, that's not it. You would not believe how many lawbreakers want to get out of a ticket. Many of these women will lose their license if they get one more." Then he exaggerated a few more war stories on what a great lover he was and even more regarding the control he had on the women in the area. It was all Jim could do to keep his anger under control—or to laugh. Finally, they stopped in front of a building that looked like an old trading post. The sign over the front porch read "Kurt's Gun and Supplies."

"Kurt's a real character. I think you'll like him."

"I hope so," Jim said in a deadpan way.

As they walked through the door Kurt called out, "What can I do for you boys today?"

"Jim here wants you to make him a deer rifle out of this Springfield."

"Boy, can you handle a 30-06?"

"I used to shoot my dad's. It kicked like hell but it hit what I aimed at."

"Yeah, well, and it'll kill what you hit, too."

Getting out of his chair with a bit of effort, Kurt said, "Let me see the rifle. When do you want it back?"

"He needs it for deer season," Billy Bob chimed in.

"That's just two weeks away!" Kurt said.

"Well, can you do it?" Billy Bob said in an insisting way.

"No, not really. But I just converted one of my own. If you want to trade guns, I can let you have that one."

"What's it going to cost Jim?"

"His rifle and $50." Kurt waited for the reaction.

"Wow, that's a little steep."

"Because he is your friend, I could let it go for $45."

"If you will mount the scope for me I will give you the rifle and forty dollars."

Kurt stuck out his hand, "It's a deal. I can't mount it until the weekend, however. That'll be okay, won't it?"

"Yeah, I'm coming down here for Mr. Bob next week anyway," Billy Bob said. "I could pick it up then."

"Great, looks like I get to hunt, thanks," Jim said.

"Let me see that scope of yours."

Jim walked out to the car and retrieved the large paper bag. He pulled out the scope wrapped in the towel. When Kurt saw the scope he let out a long whistle. "Son, where did you get this scope?"

"It was a bonus on the last job I had."

"Your boss must have really liked you!" Kurt said.

Billy Bob said in a curious way and aimed at Kurt, "Why do you say that?"

"Son, do you know how much a scope like this costs?"

"No, sir. I don't. Is it much?"

"You can buy a car for less."

A little jealous, Billy Bob asked sheepishly to cover up his lack of knowledge concerning specialty riflescopes, "What's so special about it?"

"Well, first it is adjustable from 4 to 12 power, but best of all it was built to collect light, almost of night vision quality. If you had a full moon, you would see through the scope like it was daytime. That will be great for those big bucks that only come out at dark. Boy, will they be surprised. Son, it's a shame you are putting this scope on a fifty dollar rifle."

"Forty dollar rifle."

"Yes, a $40 rifle."

"Won't the rifle do the job?"

"Oh, it will get the job done. It's just like putting a Rolls Royce radiator cap on a Chevrolet. It does the job but it sure looks strange. Son, do you mind if I shoot it a few times after I mount it?"

"No, sir. Shoot as many times as you like."

"What distance do you plan to zero it?"

Looking at Billy Bob to get his approval, Jim said, "What do you think? A hundred and fifty yards?"

Still a little jealous, he was caught off guard by the question. "I guess that will be good, yeah, make it a hundred and fifty yards."

"Is that a grocery store next door?"

"Yes, sir, it is. Old man Turner runs it."

"Billy Bob, I'm going to get me a couple of apples for the ride back. Do you want one?"

"Sure, but we can stop for lunch on the way home."

"We can still do that, just need a snack to tide me over. I'll be right back." He left quickly before Billy Bob could reply.

As he walked in, Jim saw an old man who looked like he was in his seventies. Picking up his apples, he said, "Are these apples good?"

"They tell me they are. Don't know myself. I can't eat them with my new teeth. Anything else you need?"

"No, sir."

"That'll be eighty cents."

"Sir, I was wondering if I could ask a favor."

"What's that?"

"I'm going to be out of town for a few months and won't be able to send a letter to my grandfather. I send him one every two weeks. He looks forward to those letters coming in and I don't want to disappoint him. Could you send one of these every two weeks? I've written three. That should be enough until I get back."

"Son, it's nice to see a youngster taking care of his grandfather. Give me those letters. Which one do you want mailed first?"

Jim marked them and thanked him again.

Walking up to the door he threw an apple to Billy Bob and said, "The old man said they were great apples." Then he threw one to Kurt.

"Jim, are you ready to hit the road?"

"Guess so. Anything else you need Kurt?"

"Nope. Your rifle will be ready next week. Send me a picture of what you kill."

He thought for a minute and then said, "I'll try—if I can hit anything."

Billy Bob said, "When can you have the Springfield converted? I think I need one."

"December, at the earliest."

"See you next week," Billy Bob said.

"So long."

On the way back to Blue Ridge Billy Bob kept pushing for information on the scope. Jim steered the conversation back to Billy Bob's love life, all the while saying to himself that Billy Bob wasn't as stupid as he looked. With his ego getting the best of him, Billy Bob took the bait like a largemouth bass.

After being on the road for almost an hour, Billy Bob's stories began to dry up. For a while there was silence in the car, strange silence.

"How did it feel to shoot someone?"

For a moment Billy Bob didn't respond. Jim was afraid at that point he had pushed it too far, that the newfound friendship would not stand for such an intrusion.

"Strange at first, like it was happening and I had no control over it. When it was over, I had a rush you wouldn't believe."

"Were you afraid afterwards?"

"Oh, yes, until I called Craig," Billy Bob said, smiling.

"What did he do?"

"He told me I shot her in the line of duty, to be proud of what I had done. Then I knew everything was okay."

"What made her try to kill you?"

"I'm not sure. All I wanted was a piece of ass. Craig had been tapping it for a while, so I figured it was time I got some. Her daddy was a drunk anyway. It was on a Saturday when he was rip-roaring drunk, couldn't count to three. He ran his truck off an embankment and into the church cemetery. I was the first one to find him. The old man was too drunk to get hurt so I threw him in the backseat of my car. He stayed passed out. I decided it would be worth some of Miss Susie's time to keep me from locking up her old man. Got the picture so far?"

"What did she do?"

"Oh, at first she was all for it. She said that sex was all Craig and I thought about. She pointed to her bedroom and said let's get it over with. Then it happened."

"What?"

"While I was taking off my clothes she jumped up from the bed and said she would be right back. She came back all right—with the biggest knife I ever saw. She screamed you will never want another woman and then she came after my manhood. I found my pistol and yelled for her to stop. When she saw the weapon, rather than backing off, it was like she became a wild woman. Each time I shot her she would stop for a second then come after me again with the big knife. I'll never know what made her so crazy. But, hey, you know what's funny?"

"No, what?"

"Craig told me later that it was a good thing I didn't screw her because, if I had, I would've got the clap. He told me that was why he didn't fuck her anymore."

"Boy, you were really lucky."

"Yeah, that VD is bad shit!"

Billy Bob eventually parked in front of the city jail.

"I'll pick up your rifle next week. Gimme a call on Thursday."

"I'll do that. Thanks so much for the ride. Had a good time," Jim said, concealing his disgust.

"See ya'. Gotta check in," Billy Bob said.

"Later—"

The next morning Mike wanted to know if he had a good time. He assured him he had a great time and that the lobster was delicious. He also mentioned to Mike that his friend was getting a promotion and might be moving to Texas or California. He let Mike know that when his friend moved the man planned to build his own house and had asked him for some help.

"Are you going to leave us?"

"Well, maybe for a couple of months."

"That should be fun for a while anyway," Mike said. "Let's go get some of Judy's coffee."

"Sounds great!" He felt good when he was with this old man.

13
Finding Magic

SATURDAY MORNING, HE WAS UP before daylight and so excited there was no way he could get back to sleep. All he could do was think about Peggy. Would she be there tonight? Nick seemed to think so. He prayed Nick was right. Then a cold chill ran down his spine. What will he do if she is there? He didn't have a car; he didn't even have a driver's license. What would he say, something like, "Can I walk you home, twenty-five miles to Jasper?" Don't think so! *What makes you think she wants to be alone with you anyway,* he thought. *If she is there tonight then maybe I have a chance. If she isn't, then I know she doesn't feel the same as I do. Be patient,* he told himself.

Mike closed the window of the post office just after noon. Going to his apartment, he took a shower and put on fresh clothes.

Instead of walking directly to the supper club as he normally did, he walked in the direction of Mr. Bob's house, crossed the street from the post office and to the sidewalk that marked the boundary of the yard. The sidewalk ran north and south, with a set of steps in the middle of the block that joined the walk leading to the front porch. It looked as if it had never been used. He continued on until reaching the edge of the yard on the north side, turned left, which was west, on the sidewalk that led to the elementary school. The yard bordered the sidewalk almost three-fourths of the way. At the end of the yard was a dirt road that ran south, just behind the house and joined the sidewalk on the south side of the yard.

Jim thought that was strange. A well-manicured lawn with a concrete sidewalk on three sides, with an impressive lay of cement in the middle should have more than a dirt road leading to the house. Behind the road was a small strip of woods that prevented anyone from seeing the house from the rear. The trees also blocked the view from the school. He was sure that was Mr. Bob's idea.

He continued up the sidewalk until he reached the school. Then he turned south looking for a possible route through the woods. He was pleasantly surprised to see that over the years the kids had made a path they could use and not be seen by anyone in the house. He followed the path to the south side of Mr. Bob's yard.

Deciding he had learned enough today, he continued south to McKinney Street, turned left and began his walk to the tavern to see his friend, Nick, and, more important, to see if Peggy would show.

It was a beautiful fall day with the trees taking on the colors of a rainbow. What made it more impressive was the leaves were so bright it was hard to look at them in the sunlight. He didn't remember leaves being this brilliant in his hometown. He thought these North Georgia Mountains do have a special charm or maybe he had just never noticed the colors before. He wondered if Peggy liked the fall colors. In fact, he wondered about the things she did like besides dancing. He had never met anyone who liked to dance as much as she did.

Nick was in his usual place when he arrived. He filled a frosty mug with beer and slid it to him across the bar top. "Come to see if your plan worked?"

"Yes, sir. You know a guy has to follow fate."

They started talking until the usual crowd began to arrive. Then he moved to a booth where he could see the front door. Time went by, song after song. But eventually, he couldn't believe his eyes. Suddenly there she was. He looked at his watch and it wasn't 8:30 p.m. yet. She was early and it looked like she was alone, a good sign. He was paralyzed and couldn't get his feet to move or his brain to sort out what was going on. Why did she have this effect on him? All he could do was look her way and smile. She made a quick scan of the room and saw his big smile in the corner booth. As she started his way someone grabbed her by the arm and pulled her to their table. His heart stopped, but she quickly recovered and continued on to his booth.

"Hi, there, stranger!"

"Evening, ma'am."

"You ready to dance, cowboy?"

"You know it!" Jim said, but was all he managed to say.

After a couple of fast dances, they sat down with a couple of beers to cool down.

"Do you think I'm good looking?" she said, looking straight into Jim's eyes.

"Oh, no! Here you go again. Do you always say what's on your mind?"

"Guess I do," she said.

"I know it saves time and, yes, I do"

"Do what?" she said, smiling.

"Yes, I think you're beautiful, but you know that. Why did you ask?"

"Just wondering. Are you playing hard to get or are you just not interested?"

"What if I say I'm playing hard to get?"

"Well, if you are, it's working," she said.

"Now that you know I'm interested, are you going to dump me?"

"No, silly. I'm going to show you the submarine races," she said with a newfound energy.

"Submarine races?"

"Oh, yes. They race every night on Blue Ridge Lake. Interested?"

"Yeah."

"Then let's get out of here."

They walked outside to her car. She opened the door saying, "Get in."

"Is this your car?" Jim said, a bit surprised.

"What do you think?"

"I'm surprised to see you driving such an expensive car."

"Yeah, you don't see many school teachers driving a baby blue Buick. Got a deal I couldn't refuse."

"Deal?"

"Graduation gift from my father," she said.

"He must be a nice man."

"Not really. We haven't spoken in, well, what is it, over three years, I guess."

"Sorry."

"That's okay."

"Tell me about these races," Jim said.

"Just be patient, dearest. I think you'll like them."

She drove through Blue Ridge and out of town on a crooked and twisting road that led to nowhere he had been. She made a steep turn to the left. This caused him to slide up against his door.

"That's dead man's curve," she said.

"I can see why they call it that."

A half of a mile later she turned onto a well-used dirt road. After a few minutes she turned onto an even smaller road. Then without warning she pulled up behind some bushes and stopped, turning out the lights and shutting off the engine.

"Is this it?"

"Yeah, what do you think?"

"I think you just wanted to get me alone! In South Georgia we call this parking."

"We do, too," she said smiling as she slid across the seat until her face was only inches from his. "What do they do when they go parking in South Georgia?" Without saying a word he pulled her to him giving her a long, slow kiss. It was the kiss he had been dreaming about for weeks! When they parted they were both out of breath. She whispered, "My God, that was good." For the next ten minutes they didn't even come up for air. Then they relaxed in each other's arms, smiling.

"I knew you were something special the first night I saw you."

"I didn't think you knew I was alive."

She pulled his face to her lips. "What do you think now?"

For the next few hours they talked, kissed, talked, kissed and held each other as if they were afraid the other would get away.

"I'm hungry. What time is it?"

Looking at his watch, he said, "It's 2:00 a.m. It's past my bedtime."

"Jimmy boy, are you complaining?"

"No way! In fact, when can I see you again?"

"Want to see me again, huh?"

"I really don't want to let you go anywhere."

"Good answer."

They talked as she drove them straight back to his apartment. "How do you know where I live?"

"Remember you said you lived over the post office? Well, this is the only post office in town."

"I can see why they made you a teacher. You sure don't kiss like a teacher, though."

"And how does a teacher kiss?"

"I'm sorry I brought it up!"

"Good answer."

"Miss Peggy, do you know I don't even know your last name?"

"Do you always kiss women you don't know?"

"Honey, be serious. I'm embarrassed that I don't even know your name."

"It's Taylor."

"Glad to meet you, Peggy Taylor. You kiss good, too."

"Just good?"

"Okay, maybe great. When are you coming to the big city of Blue Ridge again?"

"When do you want me?" she said.

"Tomorrow."

"I can't tomorrow, but how about next Friday? I could pick you up here."

"It's a date."

Jim pulled her into his arms and sighed, "Tell me you feel the same magic I feel."

"Magic, that's it exactly. Magic. Oh, yes, did I ever—"

After she left he couldn't sleep. Sitting at the kitchen table he was surprised to see the sun break over the mountains and all he had thought about for hours was Peggy Taylor.

14
Mr. Bob & Craig Foster

JIM COULDN'T WAIT FOR THE Barkleys to open the post office on Monday morning. They saw him smiling as soon as they got out of the car.

"What happened? Why are you so happy? Did you find a lot of money?"

"I met the most wonderful woman on the planet. She's a schoolteacher in Jasper. She said she used to live here in Blue Ridge."

"Does this wonderful person have a name?"

"Yes, ma'am. Her name is Peggy Taylor."

"That name doesn't ring a bell, she must be one of the Taylor girls that lived on the hill behind the courthouse."

"I'd like to take you both to McKinney's Café for lunch to celebrate."

They both laughed and said they'd go, but they would pay for their own lunch."

"Oh, no. Please let me treat you."

Reluctantly they agreed. When 11:30 arrived, he went to the back of the post office to get them for lunch saying, "It's time to go."

"Why so early?"

"I want us to get a good seat."

Mike said, "I guess we better go before the boy busts a gut."

They were the first customers in the café and took the table up front, in the corner. The view was the best in the room. Not only could they see everyone in the café but they could also see the people on the street. Mrs. McKinney, the owner, came over to take their orders and Mike joked with her about Jim's new girl. It made him feel like he truly belonged. Then the door opened and an older, distinguished man dressed in a nice, well- tailored suit came in with a big, ugly black dog.

"Mr. Bob! You can't bring that dog in here," scolded Mrs. McKinney.

"This dog goes where I do," he stated.

"You'll get me in trouble with the law," Mrs. McKinney said.

"How about that stuffed eagle?"

"If you stuffed that dog no one would complain!" she said, only half kidding.

"You let me worry about the law. Just go fix me some green beans and new potatoes. That's your special on Monday, isn't it?"

"Is there anything else?" she said.

"I'll order more when my son arrives."

Just then another couple came in taking a table next to theirs. Just as the café settled down, in came a tall, thin man with carrot red hair. Jim had never seen so many freckles on anyone. The man started to sit down at Mr. Bob's table when he noticed Mike. He came across the floor towards them.

"Ma and Pa Barkley. How's your hammer hanging, ol' man?"

"I'll live."

"Who's your friend?"

"This is Jim Cole. Jim, this is Craig Foster," Mike said.

"Have they told you who I am?" Foster said.

When Jim heard the name, the information from the letter came rushing back. Anger from deep inside him almost exploded. He wanted to kill this man or at least lash out and throw him through the window.

"Oh, yes. You're the one that was supposed to join the Army with Michael and then turned chicken."

Craig's face turned red. He stood silent for a moment then he came back with, "It's a good thing I didn't. Look what happened to Michael." Turning quickly and not allowing a response, he walked away. Jim realized only after the encounter that what Foster said could have really hurt the Barkleys.

"I'm so sorry. I shouldn't have said that."

"Don't worry son. It needed to get out," Mike said.

They ate their meal in silence. The joy was gone from the celebration all because of the arrival of Mr. Bob and Craig Foster.

The next week dragged by. He tried to fill the hours. In the afternoons he watched the children on their way home from school. However, they had changed their route to the other side of the street. It looked as if Mr. Bob had won the war. *Not for long,* he thought to himself.

As he watched the dog and its' owner, really watched and noted all regularities, he realized they had developed certain habits, predictable, consistently so. He noted when Mr. Bob walked the dog, when he let him run free and any time the dog was outside for any reason or time of day. Definite patterns clearly emerged. *It's almost time... It's almost time... Time for Mr. Bob to suffer a little pain,* he thought. *Yeah, a little pain.*

Jim decided to delay no longer, time to get his supplies together. When Mike locked the post office window, he climbed the stairs looking for his list. He knew it was time to buy the boots, compass, raincoat or something to wrap his rifle, soon to be in his possession. He opened the hidden compartment under his bed and took out four twenties from the roll of money he had stashed when first arriving. This is what he was born to do.

15

Equipment

JIM EASED DOWN THE STAIRS and turned down Main Street, towards Johnson's Bait. The fishing equipment was located in the back, groceries in front. He saw what he was looking for—knee-high rubber boots. He picked up a pair. Mr. Johnson asked him if he could help.

"Yes, sir. I need a pair of boots. How do you tell the size?"

"Turn the boots upside down, the size is printed on the instep. What size do you need?"

"Nine and a half or ten."

"They only come in even numbers, so you'll need a ten."

"Do they come in boxes?"

"They come just like you see them, tied together," Mr. Johnson said.

Jim found a pair of size elevens and set them aside. He then saw a pair of all rubber-fishing waders. They were the kind with no boots, really just rubber socks. You would need to wear tennis shoes to prevent them from getting holes from rocks.

"How much are these waders?"

"Son, I hate to see you waste your money. Any briar you hit going into the creek will put holes in them. That's my last pair. I won't let that salesman bring any more in here. If you really want them, how about an even $7.00?"

"I'll take 'em."

"What else can I get you?"

"Do you have a compass?"

"No, why do you need a compass?"

"To keep me from getting lost! I'm new to these mountains."

"Everyone knows if you get lost in these mountains just walk downhill until you find a stream and follow it until it comes to a road."

"I'll remember that, but I'd feel better with a compass. Used one when I was a Boy Scout."

"Well, the only place in town to find one would be Lovell's 5 & 10 or Mull Department Store. Mull's sells Boy Scout uniforms and equipment. Only scouts use compasses around here."

Jim paid for his equipment and left, thanking Mr. Johnson for his advice.

By the time he had walked back to town, Lovell's and the department store were closed and he decided to pick up the other items during lunch on Friday—so far, so good.

The next day when he was making the coffee run for Mike he called Billy Bob to check on his rifle. The same secretary answered and before she could ask the question, "I need to talk to Billy Bob about hunting."

"I'll put you through."

He identified himself when Billy Bob answered and asked if he had visited Kurt.

"Yeah. I've got your toy in the trunk of my car."

"Great! Would you mind keeping it for me for a while?"

"No problem. Why don't we go out Saturday and zero the scope?"

"That would be wonderful. I can meet you at the jail around 1:30 p.m. I need to buy some ammo. Where can I get 30-06 shells?"

"Western Auto, directly across from McKinney's Café. If you'd like, I can pick up a box for you."

"If it wouldn't be too much trouble."

"I'm going there in a few minutes to get more ammo for my .243 anyway."

"Thanks. Would you get me a box of 180 grams 30-06?"

"Wow! Going top of the line, huh?"

"I hear deer are really hard to kill and I want a bullet that'll knock 'em down."

"Well, 180 grams will do that all right, but with your light rifle it's going to kick like hell," Billy Bob said with some surety.

"See you Saturday afternoon at 1:30," Jim said. "Have a good one."

16

Falling in Love

JIM FINALLY COMPLETED HIS LITTLE chores as the week came to a close. It was Friday night and he was feeling like a schoolboy again. Showered and dressed in record time, he couldn't decide if he would meet her in the room or on the street. He went up and down the stairs five times before he decided to sit on the bench in front of the post office until she arrived.

The second hand swept across the twelve at exactly 7:30 p.m. and the Buick turned the corner. With a big smile, he stood and waved her over. He couldn't believe how happy seeing her made him feel, just the sight of her smiling face. This wonderful creature was getting under his skin—big time.

She pushed open the passenger door and said, "Get in. I'm hungry. Let's get something to eat."

He jumped in, closing the door behind him. As he did she stepped on the gas and they quickly left town. Without warning she pulled off the highway, into a church parking lot. Turning off the engine, putting it in park, she slid across the seat to kiss him with a passion he had never seen before, from anyone. All this happened so quickly that he was breathless. She moved back across the seat, cranked the car and pulled back onto the highway.

"Hey, Mr. Jim Cole. I missed you."

Those words were music to his ears.

"I missed you, too. Where are we going?"

"Harry's Steak House, next to Lake Blue Ridge Dam."

"A steak and baked potato sound like heaven to me."

"I have been thinking about a steak all the way from Jasper. At first I thought I would eat and then get my kiss, but when I saw my shy guy waving at me, I couldn't wait."

"I don't think I will ever get used to you saying exactly what you feel. I know it's, well, refreshing, but sometimes it scares the hell out of me."

"Why? Isn't it what you want to hear?" she said.

"Yes, it's exactly what I want to hear. I just don't know how to answer you."

"Don't worry. You don't always need to answer me."

"That's good to hear. Now I can breathe again."

Pulling into Harry's parking lot, it was almost empty.

"I'm hungry. Does that scare you shy guy?"

"Do teachers insist on being in control all the time?"

"Ouch! Shy guy, I thought you didn't know what to say! Come here, put your arms around me and tell me you missed me. Yes, we need to be in control because if we are not someone may just see how scared we are."

"Do I scare you?"

"To the bone," she said, a truth he didn't fully yet comprehend.

He pulled her close, kissed her long and hard and then whispered in her ear, "I will never let anything happen to you. I promise." He hugged her again, "Let's go eat."

They walked into the upscale restaurant and looked about, seeing mostly couples with a few foursomes. He thought he was a little underdressed as many of the men wore sport coats. She noticed his hesitancy, "Is something the matter?"

"It looks like I should have worn a coat".

"Just wait. These are the businessmen from Blue Ridge. Wait 'til the usual crowd gets here. You'll feel right at home."

They enjoyed their steaks. She had ordered a filet mignon, medium well, and he had opted for a porterhouse, well done. The cook was a magician, and the steaks were perfectly cooked to perfection. As time passed, the more comfortable he felt. It was amazing how easy it was for him to talk with her, about anything really. When they were almost finished with their meal a woman approached the table.

"Peggy, is that you?"

"Sue?"

"Yes!"

"You look great!"

"So do you."

"Peggy, this is my husband, Sam McGill."

"Hi, Sam. This is my friend, Jim Cole."

"Jim, nice to meet you."

Peggy explained, "Sue and I went to North Georgia College together. We were roommates our junior year.

"Are you still teaching?"

"No, Sam and I have two boys now so I just play 'Mom the Housekeeper'. Are you still teaching?"

"Yes, fifth grade in Jasper."

"Thought you wanted to teach high school, Peggy?"

"That's what I used to think. There's no way I could leave those wonderful kids now. Besides, discipline problems with seventeen-year-old boys aren't any picnic. Peggy, here's my phone number. Give me a call and let's catch up. Okay?"

"Sounds good, and I will. Wonderful to see you. Jim—"

"Good night," Peggy said, and Jim nodded.

After the couple left, Jim said, "Looks like you have friends everywhere."

"Is that bad?"

"No, I think it's wonderful. You have so many close friends. I'm envious." After taking care of the check and leaving a tip, they walked to the car hand in hand.

"Where are you taking me now?" Jim said.

"Home."

"Home?" Jim asked.

"Yeah, I want to see what you have done to the apartment."

He wasn't sure he was comfortable with Peggy in his apartment. "You don't look pleased," she said.

"I'm just not sure it's clean enough to entertain."

"Sure, sure. You just don't want to be alone with me!"

"Lady— I'll show you the moon! Let's go."

He was nervous as they climbed the stairs to his apartment.

"You've moved things. It looks good," she said.

"How do you know I moved things?" Jim wondered. "Have you been here before?"

"Oh, yeah. Many times, when Michael lived here."

"Did you know Michael?"

"He and my brother were in the same group of friends. I had a major crush on him when I was a freshman in high school. Michael didn't even know I was alive. He was in love with Susan."

Then she threw her arms around him.

"When are you going to kiss me?

He didn't say a word, just reacted. The deep, emotional feeling he had a week ago was back. Holding her tightly he felt like he had been stuck by lightning. He had to fight himself to keep from ripping her clothes off. His desire for her was almost unbearable. He knew instinctively that going slow and cautiously was the best route to take with her. He sensed that sometime in her past she had been hurt emotionally, though he could be wrong. With this deep feeling for this woman he knew if he were not patient with her he could lose her. It made him sick to his stomach to think what that would do to him.

He kissed her again, and again. They both seemed to have the same feelings, as they just couldn't get close enough. The more they held each other the more they wanted to be just one person. He kept fighting his urge to overpower her and make love to the most beautiful person he had ever seen. His frustration level was climbing to the rafters. This patience approach was frustrating her too. So much so that she took his hand and guided it to her breast.

"Please touch them. They ache for you."

He responded by kissing her on her neck and moving down her body until he was kissing her breast. Her breathing became very labored. She loved what he was doing and let him know it. Before he realized it, she had moved his hand down to her knee. As he moved it up the inside of her leg, she responded by spreading her legs to aid him in his pursuit. However, his hand ran into a major obstacle—she wore some kind of garter belt. The discovery of the garter belt and girdle assemblage achieved its purpose. It put a clamp on his passion to a level where he could control it. He eased up on his embrace and stepped away, starting a conversation. She seemed to recover more quickly than he.

"You sure do make me feel like a woman. If I don't leave, you might not respect me in the morning."

"I agree. I never want to do anything that would offend or hurt you in any way. Why don't we take a break until tomorrow?"

"I'm sorry, but I need to do something tomorrow."

"Oh, I see. You set my body on fire and then just leave me, cold, out in the snow," he teased.

"No, that's not it. Remember the friends I was with at the supper club? Well my friend and I always go to the supper club at the end of the month. We also all go to Canton the second Saturday of each month. Tomorrow is the second Saturday. I, too, never want to hurt you. I hope you understand."

"I know a promise is a promise. When do I get to see you again?

"How about Sunday?"

"Sounds good."

"We can go on a picnic. Have you been to Hogback?"

"Hogback, are you pulling my leg?"

"No, silly. There is a place named Hogback. It's a ridge that allows you to see the same river on both sides."

"That sounds like a special place. I can't wait."

"I guess I should get home."

"I don't want you to go, but I understand. Be careful. Watch out for Billy Bob. I understand he likes to pull women over and collect a fine."

"I know Billy Bob and he knows better than to pull me over."

"He does?"

"Yes, he knows I'll make him a steer."

"What do you know about steers?"

"Steers are bulls without balls."

"Ouch! I want to ask how you learned that. Anyway, be careful. I miss you already."

They kissed passionately and it was clear neither wanted to part.

Saturday morning he met the Barkleys with a big smile.

"Let me guess," Mike said. "You saw that most wonderful girl again."

"Yes, sir. We went to Harry's Steak House."

"Did Harry treat you right?"

"Yeah, the service was great. Best steak I've had in a long, long time."

"When do we get to meet this dream girl?"

"I'm not sure, but soon. I want her to meet you both. She said at dinner that she knew Michael when she was a freshman in high school. Same circle of friends and all."

"Michael had so many friends we couldn't keep them straight. Perhaps I'll recognize her face when we meet."

17
Getting Ready

SATURDAY MORNING PASSED QUICKLY. JIM ate a couple of sandwiches and then packed a few things in his daypack. He folded the maps that Billy Bob had given him so he would be able to follow the route without the need to unfold it completely in the car. He knew it would be critical for him to know where he was at all times. It would also be critical to determine the quickest route home.

He put on his leather boots, deciding to wear only a long-sleeved wool shirt, and quickly walked from the post office to the city jail. Billy Bob, waiting patiently, wore his traditional brown shooting jacket. Billy Bob threw him a small brown bag as he came in.

"Thanks, how much do I owe you?" Jim said.

"Not sure. I bought ammo for me too."

"Will a ten cover it?"

"More than enough," Billy Bob said. "Ready to go?"

"Ready."

"All the equipment's in the trunk. We are going to an old rock quarry I know about."

"Aren't we going to the same place you hunt?"

"Oh, no! We don't want to disturb the deer until it's time to hunt. That will be next Saturday. Deer season's only fifteen days in North Georgia, so we have to make every day count."

After a short drive they stopped in front of a cable that blocked the road, the steel cable leading into an old rock quarry that hadn't been worked in years. The piles of trash left about proved the local people had found a convenient place to dump their larger pieces of trash, such as mattresses, tree limbs, old drums and other items. A large waste site had accumulated over the years.

The steel cable didn't seem to keep anyone out. Billy Bob took some three-foot stakes and targets from the trunk. He pointed to a bench located behind a large pile of trash. He replaced some old targets that had been used months before.

That done—he returned to the car and picked up his shooting guide. He looked at a table of numbers in the back of the book then picked up a target.

"The target's twenty-five yards away. What distance do you want to zero your rifle?"

"150 yards."

"Okay. You can zero with this twenty-five-yard target."

Taking a red magic marker out of his pocket he put a red cross on the target.

"Put your crosshairs on this horizontal and vertical line."

He pulled out a ruler and measured up from the horizontal line and made a small X. This is where your bullet needs to hit if you want it to be dead on at one fifty. Then he placed two sandbags on the bench telling him to use them as a rest and to put on the earplugs he handed him.

"Let's see how close Kurt adjusted your scope to zero."

Jim took a good rest position on the bench and squeezed off a round. Billy Bob called out, "One-inch right, three inches high."

Jim started to make an adjustment to the scope position.

"No! Shoot two more rounds to make sure you didn't move," Billy Bob said.

Picking up two rounds, Jim quickly fired at the target.

Billy Bob let out a long whistle and said, "Look at that shot group! I can cover it with a quarter."

"Just beginner's luck," Jim said. He then moved the scope four clicks to the left and eight clicks down. He squeezed off another round.

"On line, one-inch high. Shoot a couple more rounds." Billy Bob nodded his head.

Jim repeated his previous, two quick shots. "Man, if you shoot like this next week, the deer don't have a prayer."

He moved the scope down four clicks and made one more shot to check the results. The bullet cut the red X in the center.

"I'm happy—"

"You should be! Let me see if I can get .243 to shoot that well."

It was clear Billy Bob was disappointed when his three rounds shot group was twice the size of Jim's. He angrily ejected the last round out of his rifle. The empty shell fell near his foot.

While Billy Bob made the adjustments, he picked up the spent shell and put it in his pocket. Billy Bob was even more embarrassed with his second shot group, quickly making his final adjustment and fired a zero check shot. Jim's out shooting him had not put Billy Bob in a good mood and abruptly came up with an excuse to get back to his office.

The ride back to the jail was uncomfortable and quiet. It was apparent that Billy Bob was not used to finishing second when it came to shooting. He was glad to get out of the car when he finally shut off the engine. Billy Bob quickly walked to the entrance to City Hall.

"I'll keep your rifle in the car. See you next Saturday. Bring your hunting clothes."

"Is one o'clock good?" Jim said.

"That's ideal, the deer don't come out until dark."

"See you Saturday."

Jim had a real spring in his step as he walked back to the apartment. It was time to see his old friend, Nick.

18

A Good Place to Live

IT FELT GOOD TO SEE Nick at his usual occupation when he walked into the supper club.

"Afternoon, Nick."

"Howdy, looks like life's treatin' you well."

"Better than that. It's great."

"Sounds to me like a man with a woman in his life."

Feeling his chest swell, Jim answered, "I do."

Handing him a beer. "I thought so. That's great, everyone needs a mate to attack life's problems. Are you getting used to Blue Ridge yet?"

"I guess so...the pace is slow, but it's like a good place to be, so, yeah."

"I think so too. I've been here for more than fifty years. Wouldn't want to live any other place in the world."

"What do you like best?"

"Hard to say, the mountains, the change in the seasons, the hunting, fishing and most important the people."

"*All* the people?"

"Well, not all of them. The ones I don't care for I can count on my fingers. Most people in the mountains are like the Barkleys."

"Sure are the nicest people I've ever known."

"It's a shame they were deprived of having grandchildren to share their lives and love of God and country."

"Sometimes life isn't fair," Jim said.

"Not sometimes. Life's never fair. You should never forget that. Don't feel sorry for yourself or pity for others. Mr. and Mrs. Barkley are a good example. They don't worry about life not being fair and they just make every day better for everyone they come in contact with, day by day."

Nick replaced Jim's beer with a fresh one.

"Thanks, have you ever heard of Hogback?"

"Hogback?" Nick said, scratching his head. "Yeah, that's a ridgeline just north of here. The Toccoa River makes a hairpin turn and passes on both sides of the ridge. A beautiful sight. Who told you about Hogback?"

"I was invited to a picnic there tomorrow."

"Go boy! You'll love it. Anybody I know?"

"Peggy Taylor."

"She is a special lady. You take care of her."

"I plan to."

He kept his seat at the bar until the crowd started to show up. Knowing that Peggy would not be there caused him to lose interest in watching others having a good time When Nick went to the back for supplies, he slipped out the door and began a slow walk back to his apartment.

19

The Picnic

KNOWING IT WAS ONLY A few hours until he would see Peggy again, there was no way he could sleep and decided to see Blue Ridge at night. He quickly realized that after midnight the town belonged to him. Even the dogs were asleep. He walked around enjoying the peace and quiet and, after an hour or so, found himself in the school playground. He began looking for the trail he discovered on his scouting trip. Even without a light he could walk the trail easily.

He kept looking to see what part of Mr. Bob's house he might see from the trail. When he was about three quarters of the way along, he found just what he needed—a natural barrier between the trail and the house created by honeysuckle vines. He assessed the position with the keen mind of a hunter/killer—with a little pruning it was a prime sniper position. Looking around for something to mark the spot, he discovered an old red shirt that some kid had dropped months before. It was starting to fall apart but met the requirement as a marker because no one would try to salvage it. His interest in the newfound mission helped stop his constant thoughts of Peggy and with this distraction came the desire to sleep.

It was almost 3:00 a.m. when he got back to the apartment and dropped off to sleep.

He opened his eyes to the sound of someone knocking on his door, looked at the clock and saw that it was 9:00 a.m. He had overslept!

Getting dressed quickly, he went to the door to find the most beautiful woman he had ever seen. He was embarrassed.

"I let you have one free night and you party all night."

He didn't know what to say or do. She had caught him off balance and wasn't going to waste the opportunity.

Trying to be cool about the situation he had gotten himself into, he announced he needed to shower and shave.

"Do you need someone to wash your back?"

He knew he could never give the right answer so he didn't even try. She had the funniest way of lovingly needling him, to the point where he wasn't sure she was kidding or not.

He quickly showered and shaved. As usual, when he tried to shave quickly he ended up nicking himself.

"Do I need to call an ambulance before you bleed to death?"

He walked across the room and pulled her into his arms. After a long kiss, he replied, "Can I help it if you shake me up?"

"How do you feel about that fact?"

"I love it. In fact, I love you. And, no, it doesn't sound strange saying it out loud."

Tears quickly filled her eyes. "I love you too."

They just hugged for a long while, each not moving as if afraid they would break something fragile. She finally broke the spell. "Are you ready to see Hogback?"

As they got into the car she handed him a thermos. "Here. I know you need a cup of coffee."

"How did you know?"

"Because I need one."

She drove north a few blocks and after a couple of turns made way through an older residential area. Beyond the city limit sign the road turned into a dirt road. She followed the way a couple of miles, then, without warning, turned off onto an even smaller dirt road. This dirt road crossed a railroad track and paralleled the tracks to the north. The more they drove the more twisted it became.

"Some people think this road is really a cow trail."

"I can believe it."

As they drove on, he noticed that he had seen only two houses.

"Where are the houses? Where do people live?"

"One family owns the area, their houses are located some distance from the road. Each member of the family had a couple of hundred acres so they had plenty of space."

"That's a lot of land."

"See that house? You can see that house from the dam that makes the lake. That's about two miles away."

"These people have a wonderful location."

"Wait 'til I show you our picnic spot."

"How much further? I'm starved."

"Be patient, deary. I won't let you die."

She placed her hand on his knee and gave it a little squeeze. He was amazed at the warm feeling that came over him.

Suddenly she stopped in the middle of the road. On their left was a metal tower holding major power lines. A fifty-foot path had been cleared of all timber for the lines. Without the trees the view was awesome. Looking down the mountain on the right side he saw railroad tracks. Just on the other side of the tracks was a river. She pointed the river and beyond.

"Can you see that metal tower?"

"Yeah, I see it."

"That's the dam."

"Looks small," he said.

"Now look on the other side of the ridge—"

He looked down the cleared power line and saw another river at the base of the mountain. "Is that the same river?"

"Yes, it flows north a mile, towards the town of Mineral Bluff, then makes a big U-turn and comes back down this side of the mountain on its way to Tennessee."

"You're a wonderful tour guide. Looks like there's not much traffic down here. Why is that?"

"This is one spot only locals know about. We only share it with special people."

"Does that mean I'm special?"

"Let's park this car and I'll show you how special you are."

Finding the right place, she pulled off the road then opened the trunk and pulled out a huge basket.

"Let me help."

"Thanks. I'm sorry, but I'm just so used to doing everything myself."

They walked back to a location that had the best view of the river and surrounding countryside. He could hardly wait for her to put out the meal, a typical Southern picnic that included fried chicken, potato salad, baked beans. She even had banana pudding (known in some circles as *'naner puddin'*) for dessert. He filled his plate until it was spilling off the sides. For a few minutes there was silence. Then he looked up to see her just sitting motionless, watching him eat. He blushed when he realized he was eating like a starved animal.

"Jim Cole, I love you."

He stopped in mid-bite, still holding a piece of chicken in his hand. "And you can cook, too?"

He decided he needed to slow down on his eating and talk a little more. It was clear to both of them that they were completely comfortable with each other and deeply in love. They talked as if they had known each other for years.

The day went by quickly and before they knew it the sun had set. Looking at his watch he saw it was 5:30 p.m. "Where does the time go when we're together?" he said.

"Hasn't it been a special day?"

"It's been the best day of my life."

Looking at each other, they began to pack up without saying a word. It was time to go home. The ride back was much faster than the morning excursion. When they stopped in front of the post office, nothing was said as they both got out of the car and walked up the stairs. As soon as the door closed behind them their pent up passion was released. The kisses got longer and more intense. When he began to kiss her breast she began to breathe quicker. When his lips touched her nipples, she gasped for air as never before in her life.

He moved his hand to her knee and then up her leg. She opened her legs to provide him easier access. This time, there was a difference when his fingers reached the soft skin on the inside of her thigh—there was no girdle or garter. Instead he was met with damp, warm, smooth and willing skin. As his fingers stroked her panties, she held her breath in anticipation of what would come next. He realized that for the first time since he had met her he was in control. It was exciting beyond words, so much so that he realized he needed to slow down and enjoy every second but, more important, make sure she enjoyed it as much or more.

Somehow they had found their way to the bed. His shirt was gone and he had no idea how that happened. Her blouse was out of her skirt and open. Her bra was loose revealing her breasts. He paused to appreciate their beauty. Her nipples were rock hard from the attention he had given them and flushed a rosy color. One of her hands was clutched in the bedspread and the other was squeezing his arm as if she felt she would fall off the world if she let go.

He slowly slid his hand beneath her panties and used his index finger to part her curls. He couldn't believe how wet she was. As he spread her outer lips and touched her clit, she came alive.

"Oh, my God!" she said then went rigid. The base of her neck began to turn blood red and she quivered for about twenty seconds.

"Are you alright?" he said.

"I'm better than alright, you big moose! I'm in heaven. Don't you dare stop!"

He quickly removed the rest of his clothes. She pulled off her panties and threw them across the room. As he turned to her, she spread her legs wide in invitation. He quickly complied entering her in one long stroke. Even as wet as she was, she was surprisingly tight which sapped his control. Within a minute he exploded inside her warmth.

They just snuggled into each other's arms and didn't talk or move for a good ten minutes.

Peggy broke the silence, giggling, and said, "Well, now that we have the quickie out of the way, let's get serious." She slid her hand down his stomach and squeezed his penis. It shocked him that he was hard and ready to slide into her again. They spent the rest of the evening making love, becoming soul mates as meet in romance novels.

20
Finding the Equipment

T HE NEXT WEEK WAS HARD on Jim. He hadn't planned on meeting someone like Peggy, much less falling in love with her. He decided he would still complete the mission and follow the plan to the letter. That had always worked in the past. But he also made a major decision, major in the sense that this would be his last mission. A life of revenge no longer seemed as important to him now.

Monday evening was spent going over his list and finalizing the plan. He needed a timer. A slow search of the apartment revealed quite a collection of items that led him to think that Michael was probably, although harmless, a little bit of a troublemaker in his youth. The bottom drawer of a dresser had a box of firecrackers taped to the back—not the small ones, but the ones called cherry bombs, which were basically reduced incendiary devices. Remembering his own teen years, he thought to himself that a boy lighting one and flushing it down a toilet had disabled many a restroom. He wondered if they would work, as they had to be at least eight years old.

He put one of the firecrackers and a box of matches in his pocket, planning on testing them at his first opportunity. The next challenge was to find an easy way to the roof. He needed to find a location where he could observe Mr. Bob's house without being seen. He went outside near the shed and looked for a ladder or other easy route to the roof. He couldn't find either option.

A skylight on the backside of the apartment was seen but rejected as an option worthy of any choice. He decided there must be a way to the roof through an opening in the ceiling. He climbed the stairs to the apartment and searched each of the four rooms with no luck. Then he had an inspiration of no small dimension—the closet. Sure enough the bedroom closet had a trapdoor near the back. Below the trapdoor was a built in ladder. *Now aren't I the smart one,* he thought.

He climbed up and pushed open the door. It was darker than he thought it would be, and he went back down to get his flashlight then to retrace his steps. He quickly located the light switch, which turned on the two small lights, one at each end of the building. At one time the area had obviously been used for storage. A catwalk about five feet wide had been put in place to use for storing boxes.

He walked the length of the catwalk. It ran east to west with an air vent on each end of the building. He moved a large box under the vent on Mr. Bob's side. Climbing up on the box, he could see the entire front of Mr. Bob's house. He adjusted the louver in the vent. It seemed easy enough to remove and replace. He needed to check one more thing but thought he had found his observation point. He would wait until dark to make his final check.

About 9:00 p.m. he climbed the stairs to the attic and turned on the light. After coming back down he put on his jacket and began to walk towards the school. Halfway up the hill, he turned and looked back. He saw what he was afraid of—he could see the light coming from the vent. That meant anytime he was in the attic after dark, he must keep the lights off. Otherwise, everything had to be completed before dark, which might not be a bad idea.

He continued to walk up the hill until he came to the school and looked for the right location for his timer. He quickly found the ideal place. He could create all the smoke he wanted with very little damage. One more check and he would be ready.

To prevent causing any undue suspicion, he would wait a couple of days and find out what he needed to know without anyone realizing what he was up to, regardless of their position within the Mr. Bob empire. For his plan to work he needed to know how long it would take for the Volunteer Fire Department to react to a call. He only had a window of opportunity of thirty minutes, one way or the other. He needed the noise of a fire truck's siren to help cover the noise of the shot stuffed with steel wool. He decided to initiate discreet inquiries first.

This evening he would test the firecracker and recon a route into town. He put on his leather boots. He walked south on West Main's sidewalk past the new library and courthouse, turned east on McKinney Street, which crossed the railroad tracks near what looked like a hardware store. He followed the tracks south until he came to a pulpwood yard, about a city block long and well used. He continued down the tracks crossing Boardtown Road until he came upon what looked like the town's sewage plant. He walked another mile or so on the tracks, heavy woods on both sides of the tracks. The area looked as if no one had been around for months.

He searched his pocket for the firecracker and matches. After looking up and down the tracks and seeing no one, he placed the firecracker on one of the cross ties and lit it. The fuse sprung to life immediately. Five seconds later a large bang told him they were still good.

As he headed home he searched for a safe place to hide a package for a few days with little chance of discovery. When he got to the sewage plant he saw what he thought would be the perfect place. Years ago someone had stacked a large pile of used lumber. About twenty feet from the tracks, almost completely overgrown with weeds and brush. He looked down the tracks towards town, about seventy-five feet away was Boardtown Road. He only needed to determine how long it would take him to walk the distance to his apartment.

When he arrived in front of the post office, he was pleased to see it only took twenty-six minutes from the pile of lumber. Not bad.

21
Romantic Plans

FRIDAY MORNING ARRIVED NONE TOO soon with all his chores completed. His mind focused on Peggy. In the past he had never planned more than six months in advance. Now he was thinking that, after the next six months, life could begin for he and Peggy. He had come to Blue Ridge for simple revenge. He was not expecting this strange, new feeling of happiness. He now functioned in conflicting worlds.

Saturday night was the end of the month; therefore, Peggy's friends would make their monthly trip to the supper club. He wondered if she would spend time with them or time alone with him. After last Sunday he felt the latter would be the case and that gave him a rush of excitement. What could he do to make this a very special night for her? It amazed him how much he wanted to please her.

He remembered some of the books he had read while in prison on how to please a woman. He now wished he had made a journal of what they said worked best. It was obvious she came from a family that had money, so pleasing her or surprising her would not be easy. He must surprise her romantically as that was the only card he held.

All the books had sections on flowers and candles, so he decided in order to plan for success he needed to purchase those. Success meant she would want to spend time alone with him. His mission was to somehow turn the apartment into a love nest. He was caught off guard the last time she visited him. Because of passion she had ignored the fact that he lived in a dirty bachelor pad. It would be stupid of him to assume that would always be accepted.

Since last week he had taken one room at a time and cleaned it from top to bottom. He had even taken the curtains, bedspread and sheets to the laundry across from the Tastee Freeze and washed them all, twice each. While waiting he had walked across the street and had one of their hamburgers. Business was slow during the week and he avoided taking the first booth in case a teenager decided to play the latest hit by *Iron Toilet*.

While at the Tastee Freeze, he recalled his experiences since arriving in July. This Tastee Freeze was the first place he had visited, so he had a history with the place, so to speak As he ate and waited for the curtains to dry he realized he felt completely at home in Blue Ridge. Things like going to the laundry took away the temporary feelings he normally felt in the small towns he had previously selected for a crusade, as he liked to refer to his missions. This was good.

During lunch on Friday he crossed the railroad tracks to Lovell's 5 & 10. Once inside he quickly found the candle section. They had long ones, short ones, and fat ones and of course birthday candles. He selected six fat ones for romance and five six-inch white candles for his timers. As he came to the counter he asked the clerk where he could get some fresh flowers.

"Anderson's Florist across from the Western Auto, best place in town."

"Thanks, I appreciate the directions also."

It was just a short walk to the florist. Small bells chimed as he opened the door. A pleasant lady approached him with a smile that would warm any heart.

"What can I do for you today?" she said.

He shyly told her he wanted fresh flowers for his girlfriend.

"What do you have in mind?"

"I'm not sure."

"Roses are always good. I just received some fresh ones today in red, white or yellow."

"What would a dozen red roses cost me?" he said.

"You picked the most expensive flower in the shop. That would be $20."

Even though he had the money from his previous adventures, he didn't want anyone to know he had access to anything other than what he earned at the post office. He whistled to make it look good!

"That's nearly two day's pay! Let's see that's nearly $2 per flower. Could you let me have 4 for $6?"

"Is your girlfriend that special?"

"Yes ma'am, she is, surely."

"Well, then, give me $6.00 and I'll get your flowers."

A few minutes later she returned with a long box. Inside was the roses wrapped in thin green paper. He looked at each flower in the box and noted he had six roses.

"Ma'am. There's a mistake. You put in six and I can only afford four."

With a big smile and a gleam in her eyes, she said, "I never could count, a problem ever since grade school. Will you get out of here and go have some fun on me!"

After exchanging names, he knew he had found another a new friend. Yes, this town was growing on him.

22

A Hunting Trip

I T WAS FRIDAY NIGHT. TIME to lay out the equipment he planned to take on his hunt with Billy Bob the next day—rubber boots, gloves, compass, map, rubber waders, a knife and a flashlight. He had listened to the weather report all week. It was unseasonably warm this fall. Saturday's low was expected to be only 50 degrees. He would put in an extra wool shirt just in case.

Billy Bob had his weapon and ammo. On purpose, he didn't have a hunting license and was a little worried that he might need one. He would just plead stupidity and get off, like he got out of everything else. The daypack was large enough for all he wanted to take along. He decided to pack the rubber boots and put them on when he arrived at the hunting site.

With everything ready for the hunt, his thoughts turned back to Peggy and tomorrow night. He had put the flowers in his refrigerator. It was the first time it actually looked like he had anything in it. Milk, cheese, and bologna didn't take up much room. The few beers after he visited Nick didn't last more than a few nights.

His plan was to place the candles all around the room with two on the night stand next to the bed. Just before he left on his walk to the Club he would spread the petals from one of the roses on the sheets and pillow on her side of the bed. If she didn't come back with him nothing would be lost.

His passion began to grow, noticeably. He kept thinking how wonderful a time he had last Sunday. The first time was a little embarrassing for him because it was so quick, but the next two times were very slow, with him exploring her body with his lips. He discovered quickly that she loved to be teased. She also let him know he better follow through with that teasing. The time of going home frustrated was over

Another sleepless night, as he knew it was time to put his plan into action. He knew too once he started he would need to follow through to the letter if he were to succeed. In the past, just prior to implementing any of his plans, he was excited and could not wait to start. However, since Peggy entered the picture, revenge was no longer the only motivation. He was a little worried this time. Maybe there was another way.

He decided to let Billy Bob's actions decide the route he would take. The next morning crept by, only 10:10 a.m. "Are you going to see your girl tonight?" Mike said.

"I hope so, I have been looking forward to it all week."

"We saw you carrying a box of flowers upstairs. Guess you really like her."

"Indeed I do, sir."

"Don't guess about love, son. Sounds like you're on the right track. See you Monday."

He hit every other step going up to his apartment and quickly took a shower. This morning he had forgotten the advice Billy Bob had given him about no aftershave the day of the hunt. He had been thinking so much about Peggy this morning he put on more than normal. That was made clear when Mother Barkley told him he smelled sweet. He knew that she couldn't smell bacon cooking, so for her to smell it, something must be strong. His fear was that Billy Bob would take one sniff and send him home.

He shaved like Billy Bob had instructed and used Ivory Soap on his hair and body. After dressing he grabbed his daypack and walked quickly to City Hall. He couldn't afford to be late on his first hunt with Billy Bob.

As he came around the corner, Billy Bob was walking towards his police car. It seemed strange that they would take the city's car on a deer hunt, but when he asked about it Billy Bob admitted it was the only transportation he had. Embarrassed that such was the case, he climbed in and closed the door.

Jim eased the map and compass out of his pack and placed the compass between his legs so he could see it without Billy Bob noticing it. They backed out of the parking space and turned south on Main Street, passing Hall Street. At the next street, they turned right onto Boardtown Road. He recognized it was the street that crossed the railroad track between the pulpwood yard and the city sewer plant. He had oriented himself well.

"I thought we were going hunting. This road looks like a driveway to those houses."

"Looks will deceive you. When we pass through those trees we'll turn onto Bullen Gap Road. That'll take us where we're going. The road crosses Sugar Creek in a couple of places before we get there. Mr. Bob bought a couple of old farms really cheap a few years ago. People around here think you need to go to the mountains to find deer, but I'll show you that you don't. I discovered these a couple of years ago when I was hunting rabbit. There must be at least ten deer on both farms, but I only want the big buck that makes all the rubs."

"What's a *rub* again?"

"I'll show you when I see one."

Billy Bob was in a great mood. Jim felt that was a good sign, as it made his job easier.

"I have never seen you so happy. Does deer hunting do this to you?"

"Deer hunting gets me excited, but I get the happiest when I know I'm going to get a piece of ass."

"What are you talking about?"

"Last night I found the mother lode!"

"You've got to tell me."

"Okay, the high school football team played Gilmer County? Right?"

"What's that got to do with you?"

"Be quiet and I'll tell you. It seems one of the cheerleaders' friends drove down to Gilmer County in Daddy's car The football team and cheerleaders are required to ride the school bus but three of them decided to ride home with this girl. Some of the ball players were going with them. As luck would have it, the coach caught them slipping off the bus and axed that. The girl driving had enough beer for the Dallas Cowboys. They had all drunk their share when Little Miss Shawn Johnson ran the red light next to Reese's Grocery on the north side. When I pulled them over they began to cry like little babies, begging me not to tell their Daddies. It amazes me how rich kids don't want their Daddies to know what bad girls they are. I told them driving while drunk was really serious, but being underage and driving drunk was worse. Then the one driving said they would do anything if I would let them go. I asked if they really meant *anything* and they said yes, *anything*. I told them I always wanted to have sex with a cheerleader. The one in the back seat told me to get in the car. She would have done it too but the driver said she had to get home in the next thirty minutes or it wouldn't matter anyway because her parents would catch her. Then we made plans for tonight. Two of them want to fuck me in the jail with handcuffs on. One said she was still a virgin but she would give me a blowjob. So, it's like a mother lode. Listen to this. I get a piece of ass tonight in the jail from a seventeen-year-old, a blow job tomorrow morning at 11:00 at City Hall, another piece of ass at 9:30 Monday night and the last one on Wednesday at 9:00 p.m. You know, Jan Land is only sixteen but she has the biggest boobs in the county. This will be the second time I've fucked her. I can't wait to suck her hard nipples again. You know what?"

"What?"

"I hope I don't see one deer this afternoon."

"Why's that?" Jim said.

"Because after you shoot it is when the work begins. It takes a while to gut and clean it. I want to dip my stick in something sweeter tonight, so I don't want to be tired."

"Sounds like you've got it all figured out," Jim said, a smile on his face concealing a growing hatred of the scum he was with for the time being.

"Yeah, I got two weeks to kill my deer."

It was clear to him there was no longer any doubt about what needed to be done and done quickly. However, Jim had been so sickened by Billy Bob's plans for the teenage girls he had forgotten to keep track of how far they had traveled.

"This is a lot closer to town than I thought we would be."

Pointing northeast, Billy Bob said, "See that mountain? Blue Ridge is on the other side. It's quiet out here. We will only pass two houses. People out here know to mind their own business."

"What do you mean?"

"I bring a lot of married women out here to pay their fine, if you know what I mean."

They passed over a small stream. "That's Sugar Creek, we'll cross it once more before we get to the farm."

A few minutes later he turned onto a path that was almost completely overgrown with grass, tire tracks leading to the woods.

"It looks like someone beat you here."

"Naw, I made those last week when I did a little scouting."

"Did you find anything?"

"Lots! I think I have that big buck patterned. We're almost there— hang tight. When I stop, try to keep as quiet as you can and for chrissakes don't slam the door. We'll stop on this side of the creek. Put on your boots and gloves. When you finish, put your shoes in the car and lock the door. I should have our rifles ready by the time you finish. Any questions?"

"Nope, let's go hunting."

He did as instructed with one exception. He didn't lock the door. As he walked around the car Billy Bob handed him his 30-06.

"Fill the magazine and put one in the chamber. You don't know when you might see a deer. I've killed more than one on the way to my stand before."

"That's lucky."

"Better lucky than smart and empty handed."

When Billy Bob had all the equipment ready he eased the trunk closed and began walking towards the stream.

"We'll walk right by the stand you will use. You can leave your rifle and equipment there. It's where I hunted last year. You'll probably see some small bucks, but I don't think you'll see the big one. If you see horns, it's legal. Shoot the damned thing. But first, I want you to see where I'll be set up. It's the best position I've ever scouted."

They walked another two hundred yards into the woods, parallel to the stream. Suddenly, Billy Bob stopped.

"This is it! What do you think?"

He looked around and couldn't see a thing.

"Where?"

Billy Bob pointed up into the tree. Someone had nailed some boards to the tree about sixteen feet off the ground. The boards made a seat with the tree as its back.

"That's neat," Jim said.

Billy Bob shushed him and smiled with pride.

"I did that last week. Squat down, do you see the bushes with bark rubbed off?"

"Yeah!"

The sun shining on the bare spots made them look white. It looked like the deer had rubbed a small tree about every twenty yards. Then Billy Bob pointed in the other direction about 90 degrees to the first. Sure enough there was a line of rubbed trees in there as well. The two lines crossed underneath the tree in which he had built the seat. It was obvious he was proud of his stand's location. Then he noticed behind and under the stand were piles of freshly cut brush.

"Where did all that brush come from?"

Billy Bob pointed in six directions. "Those are my shooting lanes. I remove some of the underbrush so I will have a clear shot. Your stand has them also. I did most of the work on your stand last year but I still needed to cut out some of the new growth this year."

"How do you climb the tree? I don't see a ladder?" Jim said out loud.

"See those nails in the side of the tree? I put them there last week. I spaced them about two feet apart so it would be easy climbing."

"What a great idea! Like going up a telephone pole—"

Billy Bob pointed out a green string hanging down from the board. "Your stand has one too."

"What's it for?"

"To pull up your rifle. You don't want to drop it when you're climbing the tree."

"You have really planned ahead. Demonstrates great foresight."

Billy Bob shushed him again and pointed out that the string had a six-inch loop on the end. "Run the loop through the sling near the gun barrel and drop the loop over the end of the barrel and pull. There's no way it can come loose."

He quickly climbed up into his homemade seat. He picked up a black strap and put it around him. It had a buckle on one end. He whispered down. "This is a safety belt, there's one on your stand too. Be sure to use it. It's easy to get excited when you see a deer and fall out."

"I will."

Billy Bob sat down on the seat and grabbed the string in his right hand. Jim held Billy Bob's rifle in his gloved hand and cautioned him to wrap the string around his hand to ensure it wouldn't slide out.

"Do you think this string might break?"

Billy Bob, annoyed, whispered, "It's a parachute cord. I can pick you up with it."

He complied with the request to wrap the cord around his hand a couple of times then began to pull on the rifle. Jim looked at the rifle and, as expected, the safety was off. As the rifle was pulled up, he kept extending his arm holding the weapon pointed at Billy Bob. When he could stretch no further, he looked up at the man in the tree. In a loud and clear voice he called out—

"Billy Bob, consider the score settled for Michael and Susan."

"Huh?" That word was Billy Bob's last as the rifle barrel released a round into his face.

The noise was louder than Jim expected. The safety belt proved its worth too. Billy Bob was securely attached to the seat with both arms and legs pointing towards the ground. The pull string was still wrapped around his right hand.

Avoiding the blood that was raining down, Jim picked up one of the trimmed small branches at the base of the tree. Looking for just the right limb, he found a section that had been dead for a couple of years. He pushed this portion through the trigger guard, testing it by pulling the rifle. The limb would not budge. The twig would break before it would come loose.

Releasing the rifle, the butt just barely touched the ground with the barrel still pointing towards the dead hunter. He looked around to see if anything was out of place. Finding nothing wrong, he walked back up the trail to the car, picking up his rifle and pack on the way. When he was twenty feet from the car, he began to worry about where he stepped or didn't step. He tried to keep to areas that had been walked on before.

He opened the car door and began wiping down any place he had touched. Satisfied that it was clean of his fingerprints, he began to look through the paper in the front seat for anything that might identify him. Stuck in his armrest was a little notebook. He quickly turned to the last page. There was the signature of four girls stating they were drunk on Friday night and had been let go on probation. He decided he would keep the book.

When satisfied the car was clean, he closed and locked all doors. With his pack and rifle over his shoulder he started the long walk back to town.

He returned using the same road they had come in on. After walking half a mile, he came to what looked like an old logging road, well used and traveled daily, so he decided he had better investigate. There might be another hunter close by who may have heard the gunshot. After walking only a hundred yards he saw why people came here. It was another convenient trash dump. He went to the biggest pile. Picking up an old table, he threw his rubber boots underneath then dropped the table appropriately so the pile collapsed covering the table and boots.

He quickly returned to the main road walking as fast as possible without drawing attention if someone should see him. As he approached the two houses on his route, he crossed over to the other side of the road and cut through the woods. Only once did a dog bark, though the dog's attention was due to other matters.

It was now almost six and just getting dark when he arrived where Boardtown Road crossed the railroad tracks. Turning south on the tracks, he quickly found the lumber pile and removed the waders from the pack. Taking the rifle from his shoulder, he wrapped it with his extra shirt and slid it into the leg of the wader. The ammo went into the other leg. He lifted the top half of the lumber pile, finding what he thought would be a dry area. He placed the rifle in the stack of lumber.

Now to beat his twenty-six minutes record to the apartment.

He was pleased as he hit the steps at twenty-one minutes, quickly showered and dressed. It was almost time to meet Peggy.

23
Special Night

A S HE WALKED IN, NICK called out, "You're late. Thought you might have gone hunting with Billy Bob."

"Would have liked to, but Kurt couldn't finish the gun in time."

"Maybe next year," Nick said. "Here, drink this beer and take a load off your feet. You look tired."

"Didn't sleep much last night."

"Sounds like a woman to me."

"Could be...could be!"

It was 8:30 p.m. and there she was, standing in the doorway, looking hard to find someone. He knew that someone was him. He began to wave like a small schoolboy waving to his Mom at the end of the first day of school. She saw him and responded with the same wave. This time he couldn't help himself. He met the love of his life on her side of the room. They folded into each other's arms as if they had been separated for months, and at that moment they were the only two people in the world. When they broke from their kiss, the dancers around them gave them a round of applause. It was hard to tell which had the reddest face, Jim or Peggy. They laughed because they really didn't care who saw them, as they were in love.

"Where are your friends?"

"Oh, they will be along shortly, but I couldn't wait to see you."

"Is this an overnight?"

"You better believe it!"

She whispered in his ear, "Let's dance a couple of slow ones and then go home."

"Sounds like a plan to me. I've never met anyone who loves to dance like you."

"Can I let you in on a secret?"

"Please do."

"The quickest way to get a woman into bed is to dance with her."

"Is that a secret?"

"Yes, every woman knows that."

"So, then, I'm wasting my time with flowers and candy?"

"You're not wasting time, but dancing is the quickest way."

"Always the teacher, aren't you?"

"That's my job."

"Is it okay for me to be in love with my teacher."

"Only if you make love to her later."

As usual time flew when they were together. Looking at his watch, he was surprised to see it was already 10:15 p.m. He whispered in her ear, "Let's go. I have a surprise for you."

"Oh, I love surprises! Can I wear it?"

"Be patient, deary. You'll see."

They quickly left the club and headed straight for his apartment. As they approached the Blue Ridge City limit sign, Peggy commented, "I better slow down or Billy Bob will have a real reason to give me a ticket."

He had a flashback of Billy Bob sitting on his tree seat like a dead cockroach. Jim smiled. "Yeah, we don't need him to spoil our night."

"Are you hungry?"

"For you!"

"I know that, but could you eat a hamburger? I think this could be a long night."

"What do you mean?"

"I guess this dancing thing really works."

Peggy parked across the street in the little parking area. That meant she didn't need to move the car until Monday morning. It was a sign to him that the night was theirs. As the door of his apartment closed, they began to kiss and touch each other like possessive animals. Then they tore their clothes off. He realized that if he didn't slow down his plan for a very special night could be lost to another quickie.

He pushed her away. Struggling to take a deep breath, he said, "Wait a minute. We are about to ruin your surprise."

"I wouldn't want to do that. What is it?"

"This surprise has rules, like Monopoly."

"Rules?"

"Yes. You must be honest at all times. Can you do that?"

"I have always been honest with you and that will never change."

"Good. Here's the surprise," he said, showing her the bed with her side covered in rose petals. Peggy squeezed his arm.

"That's wonderful. You old romantic, you."

"That's not all."

"What else?"

"You need to take all of your clothes off, put on this blindfold and lie on the bed."

"Are you trying to take advantage of me?" she said.

"Do you mind?"

Smiling, she quickly undressed and got on the bed. "What do you think?" she said.

"Put on the blindfold. This is where the rules and honesty come into play."

"How's that?"

"When I touch you, you can only respond with it feels cold, warm or hot."

"I don't understand."

"Cold means where you feel me touching you at that time has in your past felt better. Hot means you have never felt so good. Understand?"

"I think so. Cold, I have felt better. Warm feels as good as before, and hot means new pleasure."

"You got it. One other thing, if you want me to keep doing it, you say very cold, very warm or very hot. If you say anything else, I'll stop. Do you understand the rules of your surprise?"

"Yes, give me a kiss before we start. No one has ever made me feel so special. I will love you forever."

"Now lay back and here goes."

He took a rose from the vase on the nightstand and let it touch her lips. "That feels soft."

"No. Is it cold, warm or hot?"

"Oh yeah. It's warm."

"Just warm?"

"Ok, ok!" she said.

He then rubbed her ear.

"Warm."

He moved the rose down to her neck.

"Warm! Warm!"

He moved towards her breast.

"Warm, warm!"

He circled her nipple.

"Hot, hot!" she said, gasping for breath.

He moved to the other nipple.

"Hot! Hot!"

He moved back to her breast.

"Why did you stop?" she asked.

He took the rose away. "Remember; cold, warm, hot. If you want me to keep doing it say very warm or very hot."

"Oh, yeah. I forgot. My nipples, very hot."

"No, you missed your chance."

"You are not fair!"

"I gave you the rules."

"Okay! Keep going."

He then returned the face of the rose to her stomach.

"Warm."

He traced small circles around her stomach and abdomen.

"Warm, very warm."

"That's good. Now you know how to play the game." He was in heaven. Slowly he loved every part of her body. He was almost about to explode himself. He decided this time he did not matter. Her high was the only thing of importance. He knew if he blew this chance he would always regret it. He slowly guided the rose down her leg.

"Warm."

When Jim reached her knee he let the rose drop down to the inside of her leg. As he moved the rose up the inner side of her leg, she gasped, "Hot. Hot!" Without thinking about it, she spread her legs. He saw how it was affecting her and his balls ached for release. He moved the rose closer and closer to her vagina.

"Hot, very hot! Very hot!"

He traced the rose along her outer lips. She could not speak. Her hands were squeezing the blanket at her side.

"You really are a redhead."

She was oblivious to anything except where the rose was touching her.

"Very, very hot."

The more he let the rose touch her, the more excited she became. After a few minutes on her outer lips she started to swell which gave him access to her inner lips. When he touched her clitoris with the rose, she seemed to suck all of the air out of the room.

"Very, very, very hot," she screamed.

He saw the effect it was having and slowly started to move the rose back and forth across her rock-hard clitoris. She grew tense and her neck began to turn blood red like before. Her juices very quickly covered the rose. He had never seen anyone look so intensely happy. He kept moving it up and down until she quickly grabbed his hand. "No more. You will kill me. It's so sensitive there now."

She pulled off the blindfold. "A rose? It felt so soft and wonderful. Please just hold me."

After a few minutes she said, "It's your turn now."

"I can wait."

"Why?"

"When I saw how excited you were when you climaxed, I came too."

She laughed, "That's got to be a first. Someone coming without contact?"

"What did you think of my surprise?"

"Looks like we'll need a rose garden."

"A rose garden?" Jim said. "Hell, we'll need a rose plantation!"

24
The Letter

MONDAY MORNING WAS ANOTHER BIG day.
"Is this another celebration lunch at McKinney's Café?"
Mike said in a kidding way.

"Yes, sir, it is truely that. I think I'm in love with an angel," Jim said.

About 10:00 a.m., Mike called out, "Jim, here's a letter for you."

He opened it. "It's a letter from my friend. He got the job in Austin,
Texas. He still wants me to help him build his new home. No way!
He says that one of the malls in Austin has an ice-skating rink in the
middle. Can you believe that?"

"When are you leaving?"

"I don't know. He will let me know his plans in a few weeks."

"I hope you get to spend Christmas here."

"So do I." However he knew his plans called for him to be gone by then.

On their way to the café, he asked Mother Barkley if she knew
where he could buy a couple of blankets. The temperature had dropped
to freezing over the weekend.

"Oh, my, Lord! Mike, we have all of Michael's blankets in our garage. After lunch go home and get that green trunk from the garage and bring it to Jim."

He worried he might have caused a problem and began to apologize.

"Please, just let me buy a couple of warm spreads. I have imposed on you two too much already."

"Nonsense, young man. Those blankets belong in the apartment anyway. That's final."

"Thank you," was all Jim could say.

They entered the café just after noon and many of the usual customers were already there. Mr. Bob, with his ugly dog, was occupying his usual spot. As luck would have it, the table where they had sat before was open. As they took their seats, Mrs. McKinney approached them. "Hi, folks. Looks like you are becoming regulars."

"Guess we are at that," Mike replied.

"What can I get for you today?"

"What's your special?" Mike said.

"Green beans with new potatoes and meatloaf."

All three of them ordered the special with sweet tea.

As Mrs. McKinney was walking back to the kitchen, a couple entered with a small child. Mr. Bob's dog stood up and began to growl. Mrs. McKinney came running across the room.

"Mr. Bob! You control that dog or I will!"

Someone in the back of the restaurant yelled, "Get your gun, Lucille!"

Mr. Bob's face went beet red as he said, "Down, Butch!"

As the owner walked back to the kitchen, Jim asked Mike, "Mrs. McKinney has a gun here?"

"Oh, yes. I guess you don't know the story."

"What story?"

"She is deathly afraid of snakes. Some of her customers used to kid with her about the slimy crawlers. Then one day John Henry brought in a rubber snake and was going to put it on her. Well, she wasn't going to have any such thing happen to her. She went behind the counter and got a pistol. She cocked it and put the barrel in the middle of John's chest. She told him to get out or she would kill him."

"What did John Henry do?"

"He got out! In fact, I don't think he's allowed to ever come back." They all laughed.

"Guess that's why Mr. Bob didn't give her any back talk."

"Mr. Bob was smart enough to know she was mad. One wrong word from him and his dog would be dead, like all over the floor dead," Mike said.

"I like dogs, but that particular dog dead sounds good to me."

"Every parent in town would agree with you."

Just as they received their desserts, in came Craig Foster. He seemed outwardly worried. After a short discussion, Mr. Bob stood up and asked, "Can I have your attention?"

Everyone in the place stopped and focused on Mr. Bob.

"Billy Bob is missing. Has anyone seen him since Saturday?"

No one responded. They looked at each other in complete surprise. Mr. Bob turned to Craig. "Call Paul Williams."

"The county sheriff is useless," Craig said without hesitation.

"Call him anyway and the state boys in Atlanta."

Craig left without another word.

When the trio returned to the post office, Mike went to his car. Unlocking the door, he said, "I'll be back in a minute."

Sure enough, thirty minutes later he walked in with a green Army footlocker. He handed it to Jim. "You'll find what you need inside." Jim was again embarrassed as the Barkleys were taking care of him as if he were their own son. This caused mixed emotions for Jim. He moved the trunk into his apartment, planning to open it later.

That evening he sat down on his bed and picked up Peggy's pillow. He pushed his face into it and was surprised that it still smelled like them. God, he missed her. He opened the trunk and found all the blankets wrapped with a protective cloth. They actually smelled fresh. He wondered how women were able to do that. With no small surprise he found six blankets in the trunk. The one on the bottom looked old and worn and he decided he would use it to cover the vent upstairs. With the vent covered he could work at night.

He went to the shed looking for something he could use to hang the blanket and quickly found a hammer. After a detailed search, he found a box of small, box nails. He wasn't sure the nails would work. The old blanket could just tear loose. Then he saw a stack of one-inch lumber that Michael had used to stake his beans. He decided to roll the blanket around the stakes a couple of times and then he could nail the stakes to the studs—a good idea at last. He smiled with self-gratification.

He quickly put his plan to action and it worked perfectly. He noticed, too, that it cut down on the traffic noise from the outside. That gave him another idea. He would hang three more blankets and create a small, soundproof room. If not soundproof, it would at least deaden some of the noise.

Now he needed a shooting rest. The easiest way was to nail a board to the rafters and another board on top for the bench. He measured the distance between rafters at the height that would be needed and found the lumber he needed beside the shed. All he needed now was a saw. The only handsaw he could find hadn't been used since before Michael lived here. Using a chisel and oil he removed enough of the rust to make the two cuts needed.

While in the shed, he nailed together the boards that would serve as the bench. In less than an hour he had a shooting bench worthy of any sniper's dream. He only needed a seat now. He returned to the shed looking for anything he could use. The bench was at least six feet high, so he needed something to stand on. In the corner he found just what he was looking for—two sawhorses and two six-foot long, two by eight boards. If he used the barstool in his apartment, he would be set.

He was pleased with his night's work and after little sleep over the weekend he slept hard that night. In fact, he overslept the next morning for the first time since he had started working at the post office.

He didn't know what to say to Mike about being late. Mike forgave him on the spot. "We have been worried about you. You look really tired lately. Your body is telling you it needs a rest. You may be young, but you need to take time to sleep. Even people in love need sleep." Mike then let loose with one of his famous laughs.

Jim felt better when he heard Mike's laughter. He always felt better after talking with the old man. But the time was soon, and he was ready.

25

Billy Bob's Missing

WEDNESDAY MORNING, A TALL GEORGIA State Patrolman walked into the post office, looked at Jim and asked, "Is Mr. Barkley here?"

"Yes, sir, in the back. I'll get him." Jim hurried to the back room. "Mr. Barkley! A policeman wants to see you."

Barkley came into the lobby and, seeing the patrolman, grabbed the tall man's hand and shook it with the enthusiasm of a long, lost friend. "Sam! What are you doing here! Mother! Mother! Come see who's here!"

As soon as Mrs. Barkley walked through the door and saw the man her eyes filled with tears. She put her arms around him, hugging him like only a mother can. She was crying when she asked him if he could stay for a while. Embarrassed by the tears in his own eyes the patrolman replied, "I'm not sure. I have a job to do."

"What kind of job?"

The trooper then remembered he wasn't alone and introduced the gentleman with him as Walter Rodgers from the Georgia Bureau of Investigation.

"What's the GBI doing in Blue Ridge?" asked Mr. Barkley.

"Haven't you heard Billy Bob Foster is missing? Walter was assigned the case and when I heard he was being given a trooper to assist, I volunteered for the job."

"No kidding? How's the investigation going?"

"It's not yet. We just arrived. You wouldn't know anyone that might know his whereabouts?"

"Mr. Bob or Craig would be my first guess."

"They were the ones who reported him missing," the patrolman said, "claiming they have no clue where he is."

Jim interrupted with, "I bet Nick would have an idea."

The trooper, looking at Jim, said, "Who's this Nick fellow?"

Mr. Barkley jumped in. "Nick Turner, he's the bartender at the club."

"Nick Turner that was the county sheriff?"

"That's him."

"Michael told me a lot about him. I would love to meet him. Mr. Barkley, could you introduce Walter and I to Nick?"

"I can't leave the post office just now but if you'll wait until 3:00 I'll be happy to do just that."

Walter Rodgers said, "I'd like to get this investigation started. Do you know anyone else we could talk to?"

Jim asked, "Mike, would it be okay if I took them to see Nick?"

"Yeah! That's a great idea. I'm sorry, Sam, I forgot to introduce you to Jim Cole. Jim has been helping mother and me for the last few months. Jim, this is Sam Wright. He was Michael's platoon leader in Vietnam."

Jim's mind flew back to the letter written by Michael. "Sir, it's an honor to meet you."

"Same here. Do you know Nick?"

"Yes, sir. He was my first new friend after the Barkleys. Billy Bob is always dropping by to see Nick."

"Was he dropping by to see Nick or get a beer?"

Smiling, Jim said, "Not sure."

"Well, Mike if you don't mind loaning me Jim for a couple of hours we'll go meet Nick Turner."

"Go with my blessings."

"Jim, you can hop in the back seat."

As he got in he remembered the first time he rode in a state patrol car. He tried the handles and, as expected, the doors wouldn't open. He almost panicked but got a grip and began talking to the trooper about anything and everything to calm his nerves. Relieved beyond words when the back door of the car opened in the parking lot of the club, Jim noticed the building was locked up but saw Nick's car out front.

"Do you think he's here?"

"Yes, sir, that's his car."

Walter banged on the door with his fist. In a few minutes Nick came to the door.

"Jim, what's goin' on? Are you in trouble?"

"No, sir. Billy Bob is missing and these two men are looking for him."

"What have I got to do with this?"

"I told them you might know where he hangs out."

"Oh, okay. Well, come on it. Would you like a Coke or tea? I know you're on duty."

"No, sir— Nick, I'm Sam Wright. Michael Barkley told me a lot about you."

"Nice to meet you, Sam. Michael wrote me a lot about you also. He said you were his boss and that you planned to return to your job as a state trooper when the 'Nam tour was over. He had a lot of good things to say about you. He also said that you were going to help him settle a score and he might need my help as sheriff. Did you help him settle that score?"

"No. He was killed before I could find out anything about the real problem."

"That's sad."

"Yes, sir, it is. Michael was a good man."

"The best."

"Let's talk about Billy Bob."

"Where have you checked?"

"Nowhere. We just arrived two hours ago."

"Where does Mr. Bob think he is?"

"He has no clue."

"How long has he been missing, or should I say, 'away from home'?"

"Since Saturday."

"Has anyone checked the farms he hunts on? Saturday was the first day of deer season."

"No, sir. Do you know the location of these farms?"

"Not exactly. Billy Bob talked about Sugar Creek passing through them. That would mean they are located west of here."

"Can we call Mr. Bob and find out their location?"

"Sure enough. I'll call him now."

Nick returned from the phone then said, "Mr. Bob said he would meet us where Boardtown Road joins Main Street." Nick volunteered to lead them there.

"Jim, would you like to ride with me?"

Walter interjected, "That'll be good as we will need help to cover that farm."

As the convoy arrived at the meeting place Jim saw Mr. Bob and Craig waiting in a black Cadillac. As they drove up Mr. Bob waved for them to follow him. In less than twenty minutes Mr. Bob pulled down the grassy road Billy Bob had traveled on Saturday. Billy Bob's parked car stood out like a white flag. Mr. Bob stopped five feet from the patrol car. Walter Rodgers got out quickly and took control. "Don't walk around the area. I want to treat this as a crime scene until we prove differently."

Sam walked up to the car and observed it was locked. He and Walter walked around the car looking for tracks. Because of the area being covered with grass this was very difficult. Then Nick suggested they look for a path that he could take to his deer stand. As they looked around there was one path where the grass appeared to have been disturbed in the last week. It led to the creek.

As they followed the trail, Walter cautioned not to pick up or disturb anything they might find.

They eventually came to the stand where Jim was given to hunt. When they saw the first stand the progress stopped. Sam and Walter began to look around for Billy Bob. Sam found a boot track. It looks like he walked around here. Jim pointed out a track to Nick on the trail that led to Billy Bob. Nick called to Sam that it appeared Billy Bob had gone this way.

As they followed the trail they flushed two buzzards. Sam commented, "That's not a good sign."

Then the wind, changing directions, gusted in their faces. Mr. Bob asked, "What in the world is that smell?"

Grimly, Sam responded, "Only one thing smells like that, a dead body. I carried too many in 'Nam not to recognize it."

Craig was the first to see the body.

"Oh, my God! Look at him hanging up there."

Walter stopped them all with, "No one passes here. It looks like we will need a coroner. Who is that in Fannin County, Nick?"

"That would be...ah...Dr. Burns."

"Could you go get him?"

"Yes, sir. Jim do you want to ride with me?"

"Yeah. The smell is making me sick."

Dr. Burns was in his office and luckily had a light load. When he arrived at the scene he asked the trooper, "What do we have?"

"Looks like a hunting accident. The only tracks are his. It appears a small limb caught in his trigger and as he pulled the rifle up it went off. My only question is why would his safety be off?"

Nick chimed in, "I told him that would get him killed."

"What do you mean?"

"He never put his weapons on safety. He thought the safety would slow him down."

"What a fool!"

Dr. Burns had them lower the body to the ground. Sam pulled out Billy Bob's pistol and said, "Look at this. He even had the safety off on his pistol."

Dr. Burns took some notes and pronounced Billy Bob as an accidental death. Promising to do the autopsy that evening, he suggested to Sam and Walter that the inquest be held at noon on Friday. They agreed. Mr. Bob asked when they could bury him. Burns said the body could be released on Friday, so Saturday would be good. Needing to get back to work, Nick asked, "Is there anything I can do?"

"Can you drop Jim off and call an ambulance to pick up the body?" Sam said.

"Sure, anything else?"

"Yeah. Jim, tell Mike I would like to treat everyone to supper."

"Yes, sir. I will. I'll do that."

26

Fire Department

THURSDAY MORNING MR. BARKLEY ANNOUNCED to Jim that Sam would be coming by to lunch with them.

"Would you like to join us?"

"Mike, I don't want to impose and I've also got a couple things I need to do during the lunch break."

Jim truly feared spending any amount of time with a law officer who might want more details about his past that he was unwilling to talk about, idle conversation or not.

"You won't be imposing however we don't want to interfere with your plans. Maybe next time."

"Sounds good."

When they departed for the café, he followed. As they turned left down Main Street, he turned right toward the city hall. Before realizing it, he was in front of the volunteer fire department. A man about his age was washing the fire truck and this looked like his opportunity to learn what was needed.

"Hi, are you the driver?"

"No! Just a volunteer. The driver lives a block away."

"I'm new in town and might be interested in becoming a volunteer. How often do they get called?"

"It depends on the time of year."

"Why is that?"

"The fall is our most active time. The people around here burn leaves and end up letting the fire get away from them."

"Oh... I bet that makes you guys mad."

"Not really. It gives us the practice we need. Usually the fire is easy to bring under control and we get to find our weak areas."

"Like what?"

"Well, response time...just getting our people to the fire. Only a few ride the truck and the others meet us there."

"Sounds like a good approach."

"Well, we couldn't do it before we all got CBs."

"How long does it take to get the truck on the road after a call?"

"Depends."

"On what?"

"Where the driver is at the time of the call."

"Oh, I see."

"Our best time was five minutes, but we average about twelve minutes."

"I guess that's pretty good if you don't have people staying at the station."

"We think so. We all have jobs. Maybe one day we can have a manned station."

"Maybe. Have a great day."

"You, too."

Jim then walked back downtown to the Red Dot food store. Strolling in he looked for one of the bag boys.

"Do you have an extra small box I could have?"

"Look in the storage room in the back of the store. That's where we keep the empty boxes we collect after stocking the shelves."

Jim quickly found just the box he needed with the top still attached. He tipped the boy with two quarters. That put a big smile on his face.

"Is there anything else I can do for you sir?" the boy said.

"No, thank you, but I appreciate you asking."

Jim thought to himself, *This has been a most productive lunch hour.*

This was the weekend Peggy normally spent with her friend in Canton and Jim was not looking forward to Saturday and Sunday in light of that situation. He decided Monday would be the day he would start his plan. If everything went well he would be gone in three, at the most, four weeks. Still, he could not understand why the normal excitement he felt about completing a mission was not there. Could killing Billy Bob be all that was needed in this town? He would know better by next weekend.

Jim had nothing else to do on Saturday and began to clear the weeds and scrub off Michael's garden. Not only would it occupy his time, it would serve to deceive the Barkleys about his leaving. He really got into the business of cleaning the garden. Time was quickly passing by.

All at once he looked up from what he was doing in the garden and there stood Peggy all dressed in black. He was shocked to see her and first thought it was a dream.

"Peggy? What are you doing here?"

"I went to Billy Bob's funeral."

"You did? Why?"

"Oh, I'm related to him on my father's side and I felt I owed the rest of my family that much respect. You sound like you are disappointed I'm here."

"No way! Look how hard I've been working because I missed you so much."

"Sounds like you just made that up."

"Honey, I don't know what to do with myself when you are not here."

"Well, I'm here. What are you going to do now?"

"First, take a bath, then kiss you like you have never been kissed before."

"Sounds good to me, but I can't wait until you take a bath before you kiss me."

"I'll get you all dirty."

"It's clean dirt and, who knows, maybe I'll take a bath with you."

"That's a plan."

They fell into each other's arms.

"Let me get my bag from the car. Then we can take that bath."

The weekend was more heaven on earth for both of them. Too quickly Sunday had arrived and Peggy had to leave for home.

27

A Phone Call

MONDAY MORNING FOUND JIM LOOKING at the Blue Ridge newspaper, *The Summit Post*. The headline was "Local Sheriff Dies." It went on to say that he was involved in a hunting accident. The GBI had investigated the accident and found no evidence of foul play. He closed the newspaper with satisfaction, a job well done. The first part of his plan had come off without a hitch. He would begin phase two this very afternoon when he made his coffee run.

The day slowly went by and the crowd of people that hung around the post office seemed a little more jovial. It was like a morbid testament to Billy Bob. Everyone had his or her own story of some stupid thing Billy Bob had done. Jim thought it not short of amazing that prior to the death he had not heard anyone say a kind word about Billy Bob. Were these people that afraid of Mr. Bob's appointee?

The time had arrived. Jim called out to Mike, "I'm gone to get coffee."

"Sounds good."

When he entered the drug store he looked to see if they had customers. No one was around and even Judy was in the back. He opened the door and held the bell so it would not sound off, thus letting them know they had a customer. He picked up the phone and with Mr. Bob's unlisted telephone number in hand quickly dialed. Answering on the second ring, "Bob here."

"Is this Little Bobby?"

"Who is this?"

"It's your conscience."

"What in the hell are you talking about?"

"You remember that little voice that used to talk to you before Big Red died—the one that kept you straight? Well, I'm back and I plan to let you know just what kind of asshole you really are."

"I don't know who this is, but let me tell you something. This is MY town, MY county and no little fuck is going to talk to me this way." He then hung up in anger.

Jim quickly opened the front door and closed it ringing the bell and walked back to Judy as if he had just come in. Just like clockwork.

The afternoon passed quickly. Jim watched now and then to see if there was any unusual activity at the drug store. There was none. *Good, I can now make my demands without fear of discovery.*

That night, Jim opened the little notebook he had taken out of Billy Bob's car, thumbing through it not knowing what to expect. He looked for other victims' signatures in this little book of probations. He found one page that interested him. At the top was written, "Craig's Women," and under the title was a list of women's names, the kind of car they drove, along with the color and license plate number. Some of the women had a star by their names. At the bottom by a star was written, "Report any violation to Craig ASAP" There were also telephone numbers. He read through the names, but of course didn't know any of them. Except one—Sue McGill. *Isn't that Peggy's friend?* Jim thought. Her name had a star by it. On another page he found a list under the title "Mr. Bob's friends." This list had both male and female names. It, too, had stars on certain individuals. The book would require a lot of study to find major weak points in Mr. Bob's armor.

28
The Requirements

TUESDAY MORNING THE ALARM WENT off at 4:30 a.m. He dressed quickly and walked across the railroad tracks to a pay phone. Ironically, the phone was only some fifty feet from the Blue Ridge Sheriff Station, a ten-by-ten feet glass enclosure that always looked used, even though he had never seen anyone in it. Maybe Billy Bob's replacement would find a use for it.

He dialed the number listed on the piece of paper in his hand. Mr. Bob answered on the third ring.

"Who is this?"

"It's your conscience again."

"Listen, you little prick, quit calling here."

"Calm down, Little Bobby."

A dial tone was the answer.

He redialed. The phone was answered on the first ring.

"I'm warning you. Don't call again."

"Little Bobby. You listen to me, asshole. As of this minute you are no longer in charge. I took charge when I killed Billy Bob."

"You are lying! He died from a hunting accident."

"If he did, why do I have his little notebook listing all the women he and Craig have screwed? There is also a section just for you, Little Bobby. A list of the people you require a report on. I wonder what those people will say when I call them."

There was silence. After a short while, he responded with, "You wouldn't."

"Do I have your attention now?"

"Yes— Yes! What do you want?"

"I want you to do exactly as I tell you. Can you do that?"

"Yes."

"Good, because if you don't, I will take Little Bobby behind the woodshed and provide you with some long-needed pain. Do you understand?"

"Yes. Yes."

"Do you believe me?"

"Yes."

"Good, then I will run a little test to see how well you obey, sort of a proof of compliance."

"What do you want me to do?"

" I want you to get $10,000 in $20 dollar bills. Put these bills in a self-addressed, brown envelope. Then find a twelve or thirteen-year-old boy and give him $50 to deliver the envelope to the post office at exactly 4:30 p.m. on Friday. Are you writing this down?"

"No, I can remember it."

"Let's hope so. I would hate to use the razor strap on Little Bobby. Oh, yeah. One last thing—no law officers. Any questions?"

"No, $10,000 in twenties, self-addressed envelope, Friday at 4:30. Then what?"

"If you have done what I asked you will never hear from me again."

"What if I don't?"

"Then you will get spanked."

"How will I know?"

"If you receive the envelope back next week you failed the test. Now go back to sleep, asshole."

29

A Failed Test

IT WAS NEARLY NOON WHEN Mike called out, "Let's go get some lunch."

A clear November day, the pleasant temperature and clear skies made for a great walk to the café It was buzzing when they went in. After finding their normal table, Mike thought out loud, "I wonder what's happening?" When Mrs. McKinney approached the table he asked, "What's got everyone so excited?"

"It's Mr. Bob. He's having one of his temper tantrums."

"What did he do this time?"

"He had the mayor appoint Craig as the new City Sheriff."

"You're kidding! Why did he do that?"

"Not sure, something about he thinks his daughter is trying to blackmail him or something. Craig has seen her car around town a couple of times"

"Margaret?"

"Yeah, that's her name. I had almost forgotten. She left town years ago."

Mother Barkley was quick to defend, " Blackmail! Margaret would never do that! I know. She is the sweetest person I know. I love her like a daughter. After her mother died she almost made the post office her home while she was trying to make some sense out of that car accident. I haven't seen her since she left for college, but she could not have changed that much."

"I'm sure you're right."

"Mike, I wonder what Craig will be like?"

"I'm afraid he will make Billy Bob look like a schoolboy. We'll just have to wait and see I guess."

"What can I get you today?"

"Three specials will do it."

"Coming up."

That afternoon he thought about the events of the day. It was apparent that Mr. Bob wasn't complying with his instructions, must think he is still in charge. He would let the week play out and just watch Mr. Bob and Craig squirm a bit. It was clear to him that Mr. Bob needed a real attention getter. *Well, I'm the one that can make that happen,* he thought to himself. He would need to recover the rifle hidden last Saturday. He'd do that tonight.

Wednesday found Jim filling in the details of his plan. He had retrieved the rifle without incident and it was clear he would need to make a shot from the attic of the apartment. To complete his shooting bench, he would need a rest. A sandbag was perfect. However, he could not find one in the shed and decided one of the old pillowcases would work. He would fill it with dirt from the garden and complete the shooting room tonight.

Each time he had the opportunity to be outside he would sneak a look at Mr. Bob's house observing what activity he could. About 2:00 p.m. he noticed Craig driving Billy Bob's police car up to the back of the house several times. *Now what are they up to?* Jim wondered.

That night he quickly half filled the pillowcase with dry dirt, then folded and tied the case securely. He placed it on his shooting bench and climbed down from the attic to complete another needed project and placed the three white candles on the kitchen table. He needed to know their burning rate. As one candle burned he would mark the other two candles. He did not start marking until the first candle had burned for one hour. After that he would mark the others every fifteen minutes. His window of opportunity would be less than thirty minutes and he planned the shot for sometime within the first ten. He was now ready for Mr. Bob's well-deserved punishment.

The rest of the week he kept watch on Mr. Bob's house. Keeping a list on times and events, he verified that the routine Mr. Bob had with Butch had not changed. Friday, he began to get a little excited. After lunch he observed that Craig's patrol car stayed at Mr. Bob's all day. When he made the coffee run at three he noticed the patrol car was parked a half block away. From that location Craig could see Mr. Bob's front yard and the entrance to the post office. *How stupid can they be?*

A cold chill ran down the back of his neck. There was another possibility to what appeared to be their outright stupid behavior. Could he be falling into a trap? It would be dangerous to assume they were that naive. Mr. Bob had been double-dealing all his life and Jim knew that Mr. Bob would try to set him up. *Well, two can play that game,* Jim thought. He stopped looking at the obvious blunders Craig made and started concentrating on any actions that might identify him.

At 4:15 p.m., as usual, Jim began to slowly sweep and mop the lobby of the post office. He took his time trying to make it look like he was just doing a great cleaning job. At exactly 4:30 p.m. a young boy came in to mail a letter. Jim stood between him and the mail slot with his mop and offered to help by saying, "I'll mail it for you if you like."

"No, sir! I must mail it myself."

"Is that right?"

"Yeah. Mr. Bob gave me ten whole dollars to mail it!"

Jim stepped out of the way and said, "Don't let me stop a man on a mission."

The boy smiled and put the white envelope through the slot.

"Have a good weekend," Jim said.

"I will! I've got ten whole dollars!"

He finished cleaning up as Mike closed the window at the counter and locked it. "See you tomorrow, Jim."

"Good night, sir."

Jim went straight to his room, climbed the stairs, and looked about to see if anyone was watching—and saw nothing. He climbed into the attic, went to the vent and removed a louver then slowly scanned the entire area. After thirty minutes, he decided whatever Mr. Bob and Craig had planned didn't work.

He sat down on the stool, got relaxed, and smiled with satisfaction.

30
Peggy's Surprise

JIM DECIDED IT WOULD BE best to let the weekend play out with no interference from him. Besides, he had a "hot date" Saturday afternoon anyway. They had planned to see some of the area around Blue Ridge Lake and he was looking forward to the drive, but not as much as he was craving Peggy's touch.

About 2:00 p.m. Peggy parked in the lot across from the post office. It wasn't much of a parking area, just an empty lot with a token amount of gravel only used by post office customers when normal spaces were taken up. That happened only a couple of times a month. Jim watched her park from the bench in front of the post office. He had been too impatient to wait inside. It also gave him an opportunity to watch Mr. Bob's house.

Peggy quickly covered the distance from her car to the bench. They embraced each other as if it had been years since their last touch. It was as if the past week of separation had never happened. He had never experienced the miracle of togetherness before.

Peggy took up her conversation from last week as if the six days in between hadn't happened.

"My shy boy, I have a gift for you, but it can wait until later."

"Why did you tell me now then?"

"I thought I would tease you like you did me with the rose."

"Oh, is it sexual?"

"Could be, but you will just have to wait."

"You're having fun, aren't you?"

"Not as much fun as you had with the rose, but I'm trying."

"What's the plan?"

"Which side of the lake do you want to see first?"

"I'm not sure. You make the call."

"Okay, I want you all to myself today, so let's go on the south side."

"That's fine with me."

"You can see the place we went parking on our first date. It looks different in the daytime."

"I wouldn't know. I wasn't looking at the scenery that night."

Peggy laughed. "But you found my girdle."

He didn't know why, but he blushed.

Laughing, "I sure do love my shy guy. Let's go."

Quickly she went into her tour guide role. She took the same paved road she had taken to Harry's Steak House. As she made a sharp turn to the left she asked, "Do you remember dead man's curve?"

"Yeah. I remember it, it looks worse in the day time."

Shortly she turned right onto a dirt road. Pointing up the paved road, she said, "Harry's is up that way about a mile and a half."

She followed the dirt road until the lake came into view.

"That's Dry Branch Cove. See that small road on the right?"

"Yeah."

"Well, that's Jim and Peggy's parking spot."

The road curved back into the woods. He was no longer able to see the lake. After about twenty minutes the road again came back to the lake. "They call this cove Snake Nations.

"Does it have a lot of snakes?"

"I don't think so. I'm not sure how they came up with the name. Maybe in the past it did have snakes."

The road they were on joined a better- maintained road. This is Aska Road. If you turn right, it will take you back to Blue Ridge. She turned left and for the next ten miles or so they went through beautiful mountain farms.

Without warning the road turned back to the left and led to a long, metal bridge with large planks as the floor. "That's Shallowford Bridge. It crosses the Toccoa River. It's the same river that goes by Hogback. If it's okay with you, we will turn around here. If we cross the bridge we will be on the north side of the lake. Would you like to see it?"

"Not really. I would much rather look at you."

"Good answer. Let's go home. You still have a gift to open."

"I had forgotten about that!"

"I bet. Remember we never lie to one another."

"I'm sorry. Truthfully, that has been all I can think about."

"Great! Let's get home."

As usual, when the car stopped in the parking lot they would almost run up the stairs and when the door closed they began tearing at each other's clothes. All at once Peggy yelled, "Stop! Wait!"

It scared Jim. " I'm so sorry!"

"No, no, you didn't do anything wrong. I just left your gift in the car!"

"Thank God! You scared me to death. I thought I had done something wrong."

"Let me get your gift and you will see that you have done something really, really right. While I'm gone why don't you run me a hot bath? Could you do that?"

"Trust me. I think I can handle that."

She returned with a small box. Before giving it to him she opened it and took out a small bottle then handed it to him.

"You need this now."

He read the label and smiled. It was a bottle of bubble bath. He poured half the bottle into the steaming bath water. While his attention was on the bubble bath, she removed all her clothes. "Are you ready for your gift?"

"You?"

"No. Not now, maybe later. Shy guy, ever since our first night of lovemaking I cannot stop wanting you to play with me. There is no way I can tell you how special the rose was, then and always. One time you commented how long and thick my pubic hair was. Well, tonight you can fix that. Look in the box."

He opened the box. Smiling he pulled out shaving cream and a razor.

"Can I trust you not to cut me?"

Jim smiled, "I'll be extra careful. I couldn't afford something to go wrong!"

True to his word, he was careful and slow. It took him almost an hour to complete the task. Two times he had to add hot water to the bath. When he finished they could not stand any more foreplay and both worked the towel to get her dry and into bed.

After a couple of hours he whispered, "So you like for me to play with you, huh?"

"Oh no! I've created a monster," she groaned.

31
The Phone Call

PEGGY LEFT FOR JASPER AT about 6:00 p.m. That meant two things—one, he was sorry to see her leave and, two, tonight at midnight was the right time to make contact with Mr. Bob.

While he waited for the midnight hour to strike, he began to read through Billy Bob's notebook, quickly scanning each page of the book and pleased that he did not find Peggy's name. He selected three names with stars that were listed under Mr. Bob. He did not recognize any of the names but was sure they would mean something to Mr. Bob. He had two men and one woman on the list.

It was almost time for the call. He decided to use the same pay phone as the last time. His only concern was Craig coming by while he was using it. Since he had been appointed sheriff, the prick had taken his duties somewhat seriously. He even patrolled the town at night. To ensure Craig did not discover him making the call, he decided to hide near the phone until the new sheriff had passed by on his rounds. Sure enough the patrol car passed the phone at 11:55 p.m., fairly predictably. As soon as Craig disappeared around the corner, Jim came out of hiding and picked up the phone.

As usual, Mr. Bob answered on the second ring.

"Who is this?"

"It's your conscience again."

"Quit calling me, you little fuck."

"This is my last call unless you beg me to call again."

"Now why in the hell would I do that?"

"Did you get your money back?"

"Yes, you little fuck, I did. Yesterday morning. Why?"

"Little Bobby, you're getting old. Remember if you got the money back you failed the test."

"What test?"

"The test to see if you really are an asshole. Trust me! You are one hundred percent, certifiably an asshole."

"I don't have to listen to this."

"You do if you want to live."

"Are you threatening me?"

"Just making a promise, nothing more or less."

"What do you want me to do?"

"Nothing. You failed the test. Now I'm going to see how much pain I can inflict between Thanksgiving and Christmas."

"I did what you told me to do," Little Bobby said.

"You did? What color envelope did I tell you to put he money in?"

"I don't remember."

"Do you remember me telling you not to involve the police?"

"Yes."

"Then why was Craig sitting a half block from the post office."

"I'm sorry. What can I do?"

"Suffer some small percent of the pain you have inflicted on others."

"What are you going to do?"

"C'mon now, I can't give away all my surprises, but I will share one little thing. Starting Thursday I plan to call the people listed under your name in Billy Bob's notebook. You know Billy Bob was a real detailed person. He has the names and telephone numbers. I wonder how the people will feel when I tell them you had Billy Bob following them and reporting back to you? I guess you'll find out as I plan on giving them your unlisted number."

"You wouldn't do that."

"Just wait. This should be a busy weekend. Here are the first three people I plan to call." Jim then read him those names.

"When I hang up you will not hear from me again."

"Please! How can I get in touch with you?"

"By begging?"

"Please! Please!"

"Not that way, but by actions."

"What actions?"

"When you can stand the pain no longer open all the windows and doors of that big house of yours. Leave them open until I call. If one window is closed, I will not call."

"It's winter time! I'll freeze to death."

"You asked how to contact me. If you do not do as I say then goodbye and enjoy your pain!"

Jim hung up.

Monday was another pleasant day with the Barkleys. As they were walking back from the café Mike asked, "Jim would you be interested in applying for a postal worker position?"

A cold chill went down his back. What if the Barkleys discovered his true background? Would they still want him around?

"What do I need to do?"

"When we get back to the post office I will get you the application and requirements."

"Sounds good. I can at least try. All they can do is say no." Jim then laughed.

"Nonsense, my boy. Remember you have us on your side."

"I know I do. Thank you."

This was an unexpected pressure He would need an excuse to stall until after Christmas. That night he worked on his smoke bomb. He first cut all the firecrackers open and poured the powder out. On one of the firecrackers he just cut off the end. This would be his igniter. He poured all of the explosive powder into a small fruit jar, worried that there might not be enough to do the job. To supplement the supply of powder he took six .30-06 shells from his ammo box. With a pair of pliers, he removed the bullet from the case. He then poured the gunpowder into the jar. Satisfied he had enough powder, he now needed something to help with the smoke. Looking around he saw a kitchen towel. An oil-soaked towel was exactly what he needed. He smiled with gratification when everything fit neatly into his box. He even had room for a pair of pruning shears that he retrieved from the shed. The plan was complete; he was ready for the next step. The plan depended on his ability to get time off from the post office without raising suspicion.

32

The Second Letter

TUESDAY MORNING HE WAS COLD when he awoke. Looking outside, he was surprised to see the first snow of the year. It was only a couple of inches, but it was the white stuff, real snow. He remembered his grandfather would call this a tracker snow, because it was just deep enough to track rabbit; one of his grandfather's favorite sports. When Jim was young, his grandfather would take him along on his hunts. For some sad reason, when he became a teenager, he no longer had time for his grandfather. He thought that was the first big mistake of his life. His grandfather was always teaching him wonderful and exciting things, things he had never thought of before. Strangely, when he became a teenager he felt his grandfather was too old to know anything. *Why are teenagers so foolish?* Jim thought.

When he saw the Barkleys that morning they were as excited as teenagers.

"Isn't it beautiful?" Mother Barkley said, referring to the snow.

"It's beautiful, but I'm sure glad we have an inside job."

They all laughed.

"You better enjoy it now. It will be gone by noon."

"Really?"

"Yeah. That's what normally happens this time of year. The kids will be upset they won't even get off from school."

Looking outside, "It really is pretty."

He thought to himself, *Don't snow now. There is no way the plan can work with snow on the ground. How would he cover his tracks?*

Around 10:00 a.m. Mike called out to him, "You have another letter."

Jim quickly opened the letter and pretended to read it.

"From your friend?"

"Yes, sir. He got a job in Dallas. He's really excited about his new home. He found a construction company that only does framing and roofing. The new owner must do all the finishing work. It makes a new house affordable to people that can do construction work. That means he will need me for a couple of months.

"When do you leave?"

"I'm not sure yet. He gave me a telephone number he is using for the next ten days. He wants me to call him next Tuesday. He will let me know then."

"That's good. Just let us know."

"I will, sir."

33

Bob's First Pain

AS MR. BARKLEY PREDICTED, MOST of the snow was gone by lunchtime. Jim decided on the spot that now was the time to act.

"Mike I was wondering if I could have the rest of the afternoon off? I would like to check the bus schedule and do a few other things I have been putting off."

"Sure, why don't you just take off now? Our workload is really light today."

"Thanks. I really appreciate it."

As he climbed the stairs to his room, he realized the extra time would come in handy. The first thing he needed to do was finish the shooting room and went to the kitchen and quickly located the clothespins he knew were there. He put them and a pair of scissors in his back pocket and climbed back up the ladder to the attic. The only thing left to do was create a small window in the blanket that covered the ceiling vent. With the scissors he cut an opening about one-foot long. At each end he cut up and down about one and a half inches.

When this was complete he used the clothespins to fasten the blanket to the top and bottom louvers. He looked around and was pleased with what he saw.

He climbed down the ladder and retrieved the box he had prepared the night before and put on his coat and gloves. With the box under his arm he began the walk to the bus station.

He approached the counter in the station and requested a ticket to Atlanta.

"When?" asked the attendant.

"Next Thursday morning."

"Thanksgiving?"

"Oh, no, mistake, the week after."

" Sir, that'll be $12.50.

After handing her a twenty-dollar bill, she counted out his change and thanked him for the business. He then walked out onto the street and checked his watch. It was only 12:30 p.m. He went to the Rexall Drug Store and got a pack of crackers and a Coke then spent over an hour eating his lunch in the store. His best route to the school would be from the south side of the children's path, through the woods.

He walked as if he was going to the courthouse. Instead of going in, he took the street behind it. He continued to walk, passing one street, and then turned north on the next street. He concluded it would bring him out at the south end of the path.

After a short walk, sure enough, there was the path, just as he thought. He looked around and decided no one was watching. Then he moved quickly up the path until he found the shirt he had used to mark the sniper position. He removed the pruning shears from the box and completed the necessary cuts in short time. He slid the shears into his right, rear pocket. From his front pocket he retrieved Billy Bob's .243 casing that he had picked up at the range. With his gloves he wiped it clean of any fingerprints. He dropped it in the middle of the sniper position. That should help confuse the investigator.

He then picked up the box and continued up the trail to the school. Classes would let out soon and he needed to be gone before then.

Walking directly to the spot he had chosen for the smoke bomb he sat the box down next to the walk then spread the towel on the bottom of the box. Making sure he was out of sight, he then opened the jar and poured the gun powder all around the box. He then checked the time, as his plan was to make the shot at 5:10 p.m.

Jim determined which pre-drilled hole he needed to slide the firecracker fuse into and when it seemed secure he put the candle in the box in the holder he had made just for just this purpose. He struck a match and touched the candlewick. When he was satisfied it was burning, he closed the box's lid. After a few minutes he checked it again. It had a good, solid frame. All he needed to do now was to get back to his attic without being seen. He took the sidewalk north of Mr. Bob's house and crossed the street that ran by the post office. He decided the best route would be the path behind Hackney's Cleaners.

He moved quickly to the attic and began to prepare for the shot. First thing he did was make sure all of the blankets overlapped. He checked his watch it was already 4:30 p.m. How had so much time elapsed? This missing time almost unnerved him. To calm himself down he began to go through the moves out loud: load two rounds, put one in the chamber, take a good seating on the sandbag, take a good sight picture, take the weapon off safety, place the target in his sights, take a deep breath and let it out, squeeze the trigger. He was again relaxed and focused. Everything his grandfather had taught him seemed to ring in his head. His grandfather would have been proud that he had listened to him talk about when he was a sniper during the war.

He relaxed on the bench and waited for Butch to make his 5:00 p.m. pee call. Moments later, he saw Butch come from behind the house. He looked at his watch and it was exactly 5:00 p.m. Butch seemed to check every clump of grass making sure no other animal had marked his territory. He pulled the rifle to his shoulder and began to follow the dog through the scope. Then he heard the noise he was waiting for—the siren on the fire truck. It was coming his way. He put the crosshairs in the middle of Butch's chest. The fire truck kept getting closer as he waited for just the right shot. He wanted Butch to be looking away from the house. When the fire truck was approximately 50 yards from the post office, Butch turned to see what the noise was and Butch stood frozen like a bird dog pointing to a bird. Out loud, "Take a breath, let it out, and squeeze."

The bullet was gone. It struck home. Butch let out a howl, stood on his back legs and turned his head to bite the place the bullet had entered. He then dropped down on all four legs and began to run towards the big, white house. Only ten feet from the corner of the house, Butch collapsed.

Jim calmly placed the rifle on the floor and moved to the open slit and slowly looked around to see if anyone was looking his way. He relaxed when he saw the people were only interested in what was going on at the school. Jim broke out into a big smile when he saw Mr. Bob and Craig standing on the sidewalk and looking at the school.

34

Following the Plan

WEDNESDAY MORNING JIM STAYED NEAR the front of the post office to pick up any news concerning Mr. Bob and began to get a little concerned when things seemed too quiet. From outward appearances nothing had happened in Blue Ridge, and of course such was not the case. The fire call to the elementary school was not even discussed. No matter how curious he was he could not bring up any of the events. He decided he would go ahead with his plan to call the people listed under Mr. Bob's name in the notebook. After all, why shouldn't he?

The first two people he called were a major disappointment. They took the information of Billy Bob spying on them as being expected and remarked they couldn't have done anything about it anyway. For some reason he decided to make one more call before he gave up. The third person he called seemed a person of importance. It may have been only in his mind—however, he responded, as Jim would have imagined.

"Would you like Mr. Bob's unlisted telephone number?"

"I surely do! That old fart is going to pay. No one invades my privacy. I think GBI should know about this."

"Try Walter Rodgers, he's GBI and I think he's already doing an investigation."

"I don't know who you are, but I certainly do appreciate the call. Will you give me your name?"

"Just call me *Little Bobby's Conscience.*"

He laughed, "Can I quote you?"

"Please do!"

He felt so good about the last call he decided to contact every one on the list before Friday night. All he could do now was wait to see if Mr. Bob felt any pain. Based on Nick's remark about how Mr. Bob felt about Butch, he thought there would have been at least some outcry. He began to wonder if Mr. Bob could be hurt.

35

Thanksgiving Dinner

JUST BEFORE NOON, MIKE ASKED Jim if he could have a minute of his time. Worried about any possibility of being discovered, he replied in broken vowels, "What's up?"

"Mother has decided she is going to cook a Thanksgiving dinner this year. We want you and Peggy to come."

"I thought Mother Barkley didn't cook anymore."

"She hasn't in years. That's why it's so important that you say yes."

"I will be more than happy to come, but Peggy already has other plans with her school. I won't even see her until Friday night."

"I'm sorry about that. We were so looking forward to meeting her. You will come, though?"

"Yes, sir. Pleasured to. How do I get to your house?"

"I'll pick you up here at the post office at noon if that's okay."

"That's fine with me. Can I do anything?"

"Son, you have done more than you could ever know."

"What do you mean?"

"Your being here has caused Mother to wake up to life again. I will never be able to thank you enough."

That night he made five more calls, and with gusto. Only two seemed to care. Strange. He had another sleepless night. What if Mr. Bob truly had no conscience? How do you hurt someone when they have lost all their emotions?

Just as Jim arrived on time in front of the post office, Mr. Barkley drove up.

"Hop in. Mother said we'll be eating by 2:00 p.m."

"Sounds good."

"After dinner you and I can watch the Bulldogs kick WVA's butt."

He didn't have a clue what he was talking about. He thought it might be football, but he wasn't sure. When he was in high school, football was for the rich kids. During Jim's stay at the boy's home, the game of football played by the boys was jungle rules—anything goes. Therefore, football was of no interest to him, but he would never tell Mike that. The nice thing would be spending time with just the two of them. It made him feel he had a family for the first time ever.

As Mother predicted, at 2:00 p.m. she announced dinner was served by ringing a little bell. The two men approached the table.

"Oh, no you don't," she warned, "You boys go wash your hands before you sit down at my table."

Mike winked at him and said, "We'd better do as she says. Sounds serious." As they washed up, Mike again thanked him for changing their lives. Jim didn't know what to say so he said nothing.

"Let's go and chow down," Mike said. "I'm hungry."

"So am I."

The spread on the table was fit for a king and he couldn't believe his eyes. "How many folks are coming?"

"Just us. Why do you ask?"

"There's enough food to feed the West Virginia National Guard!"

She laughed, "Sit down. Let me fill your plate. What do you want, light or dark?"

"Light."

"What else, huh?"

"Are those sweet potatoes?"

"Yep, indeed! We have sweet potatoes, mashed potatoes, turkey, cranberry salad, green beans, stuffing, peas, rolls, coconut pie and pumpkin pie. You better be hungry."

"What? No ham?" joked Jim.

"Thank you for reminding me! It's in the oven."

Mike responded with one of his big laughs. As usual, it was contagious. He and Mother laughed, too. It was a wonderful evening in the Barkley home, the way a dinner should be. Jim realized now just how much he had to be thankful for, for all days to come.

36

A Planned Separation

FRIDAY, ALL DAY LONG, WAS another day without any news about Mr. Bob. He was beginning to think his plan had failed. After spending the day with the Barkleys, he was not sure he was disappointed. Maybe taking Billy Bob and Butch out of the picture was enough and he seriously mulled over that possibility.

He had completed all of his calls from Billy Bob's list. It seemed that only one third of those listed cared, cared about anything. This added to his doubts. If they didn't want to help themselves, how could he make it better for them?

When Peggy arrived Friday night all thoughts of the Fosters were put on the back burner. The time for being shy was gone. They were like newlyweds on their honeymoon. They would only stop lovemaking long enough for them to get something to eat. It seemed the more they made love the more they wanted each other. Time passed quickly for the lovebirds and all too soon it was 6:00 p.m. Sunday night, as he helped put things in her car.

As they walked out with the last load to her car, he approached the subject he had been putting off all weekend.

"I need to tell you something—"

She could tell by his face it was something she did not want to hear.

"Just say it," she demanded.

"You know my friend, Ron Creel, in Texas?"

"Yeah."

"He wants me to fly down and help him put sheetrock in his new house."

"How long will that take?"

"Six weeks, maybe a little longer, maybe a little less."

"When are you leaving?"

"Next Saturday morning."

"Why didn't you tell me before?"

"I tried. I just couldn't find the right time. I was wondering if you could pick me up Friday night and take me to the airport."

"Absolutely, but I can't get here before 7:00 p.m. this Friday."

"That's okay."

"You can spend the night at my place, Friday, and I will take you to the airport on Saturday morning."

"Will the neighbors talk? Miss Taylor with a sleepover?"

"I don't know. I'll just have to chance it," then she laughed.

She gave him a big hug and kiss. "I'm glad you didn't tell me before. It would have spoiled a perfect weekend."

"It was good, wasn't it?"

"It was the best! I'll see you Friday. Oh, by the way. I love you, Shy Guy."

"I love you too, Miss Peggy."

37

Sam McGill

MONDAY FOUND JIM STILL LISTENING for any comments about Mr. Bob. He hadn't heard anything. A few minutes before twelve, Mike called out, "It's lunchtime!"

As usual all three began their walk to the café. It was pleasant even though a little chilly. Mother asked, "Are you staying warm at night?"

"Yes, ma'am, indeed. I am. Thank you."

He liked having someone worry about him, or at least expressing out loud such sentiments.

The post office family took their normal table. The Monday special was again meatloaf and green beans with new potatoes. He had to remind himself, *I am here to do a mission and leave. Only a small part of it has been accomplished and I've let myself settle into a small town routine where I'm starting to care. That can't be good—* What bothered him was that he liked it. This small town fit. Maybe the revenge trail was over? The Long Ranger rides no more.

The front door opened and in came an old man that looked like a beggar. He went to the table as if it was assigned to him.

Jim couldn't help feeling sorry for the old guy. Then Mrs. McKinney asked, "What on earth happened to you, Mr. Bob? Where's the dog?"

"Someone shot my Butch." He put his hand inside his suit jacket and pulled out an envelope full of money. "I'll give this $10,000 to find out who did it."

Mrs. McKinney cautioned, "Put that money away! For $10,000 everyone in town will say they did it! Sit down and relax. Can I get you your usual?"

"Yes, ma'am, I would like that. Thank you!"

Jim couldn't believe his ears. Mr. Bob was actually being nice. His doubt about him not feeling pain had been removed. From what he could see he had Mr. Bob's attention and maybe nothing else was needed. He would make his last midnight call tonight.

The café quickly filled up with the normal lunch crowd. Everyone gave Mr. Bob a long stare when they came in. It was easy to see why. He looked like a destitute old man, not the richest man in the county. It was quieter than usual in the café—that much was sure. No one knew just what to say, was the problem. They wanted to know what had happened, but they didn't want to be the person who asked.

Suddenly, the phone rang breaking the silence. It seemed extremely loud for some reason. The noise surprised everyone.

Mrs. McKinney answered. "Hello, The Café. Yes, sir. He's here. "Mr. Bob, it's for you."

The silence grew thicker. Everyone was listening while trying to appear as if they weren't.

"This is Bob. Slow down. I can't understand you! You shot someone? Why? Never mind that. Is he dead? Where are you now? Don't do anything until I get there!"

He hung up the phone, put five dollars on his table and quickly left. Mike whispered, "You two finish lunch and go back to the post office. I'm going to see what's happened."

Jim wanted to go also but knew that it would be dangerous to do so and agreed to do as instructed. He watched as Mike followed Mr.

Bob out of the café and up the street. Mrs. McKinney came over to the table after they left. She began to talk with Mother. "You know, I think Mr. Bob has lost his mind, really do."

"Why's that?"

"You know it's 40 degrees outside? Mr. Bob has every window and door of his house open."

"You're kiddin'!"

"Really! One of my cooks goes by his house ever' day. Says they've been open all weekend."

Jim realized he and Peggy had been so involved with each other he had not even thought to look. Curious and anxious for Mike to return with news, the pair left the café.

Mike came into the rear of the post office looking pale and unstable. Concerned, Mother asked, "What's wrong?"

"Craig shot and killed Sam McGill."

"Why?"

"Craig says he came after him this morning with a gun so he put five shots in Sam's chest. I heard Craig tell his father that Sue had called earlier and warned him that Sam was on his way. Mr. Bob asked Craig why he was so upset. Craig reluctantly told his dad that he'd stopped her on a back road and had sex with her. Then Mr. Bob wanted to know how on earth Sam had found out about it. Craig admitted they'd thought the little boy would stay asleep in the back seat of her car. When they finished in the patrol car, the little boy came up and wanted to know what they were doing. Then evidently the child asked his dad what the policeman was doing to his mommy. Mr. Bob told Craig they'd let the judge take care of the mess and for him to keep his mouth shut!"

Mike then sat down and put his face in his hands. "It looks like Craig is going to get away with killing a nice young man and father."

Jim asked, "Why do you think Sam went so crazy?"

"It's a long story and you wouldn't know how to take it since you just came here. Sam used to work at Lockheed in Marietta. He and Sue lived here. He'd leave before 5:00 in the morning to drive to work and wouldn't get home until late. The rumor got back to Sam that Craig and Sue were havin' an affair. Sam quit his job and became a real estate agent. That was almost three years ago. Everyone thought Craig had found another woman. Guess not—"

"I met the McGills at Harry's. They seemed like such a happy couple. Why would she want to betray her husband?"

"Knowin' Craig, he had something on her and it was either give him sex or he would expose it to everyone."

"Do people in the county know what kind of man Craig is?"

"Yes, but what can they do about it?"

Jim thought every time he felt a ray of hope for the Foster family, some kind of evil crept out. *It looks like Mother was right. Craig is pure evil,* Jim thought. *Time to implement the final phase of the plan—and soon.*

38

The Final Phrase

IT WAS 11:00 P.M. AND time to call Mr. Bob. Jim nonchalantly walked to his hiding place near the pay phone and waited patiently for Craig to make his rounds and pass by. As he drove past going north on Main Street, Jim stepped out and put a quarter in the slot and dialed the unlisted number and waited for it to ring on the other end.

"This is Bob. Is this you?"

"If you're talking about your conscience, the answer is yes."

"Why did you kill Butch?"

"It seemed I couldn't get your attention any other way. Do I have it now?"

"Yes. What do you want from me?"

"I want you to try to convince me that I shouldn't kill your other dog."

"Other dog? I don't have another dog!"

"Oh, yes, you do. That mad son of yours."

"No! You wouldn't kill Craig, would you?"

"That depends on you—and Craig."

"What do you want us to do?"

"Do you have a pencil and paper?"

"Just a minute, I'll get them. Okay, I'm ready to write."

"Now listen, Little Bobby asshole. If you don't follow my instructions to the letter I'll kill one more dog this week, and won't lose any sleep over it."

"Just tell me. I promise we'll do as you say."

"Good. If you do everything I say, I promise you'll never hear from me again."

"I'll do anything."

"I'm going to let you buy your way out of this mess again. However, because you can't control your dog, Craig, the price has gone up."

"How much?"

"$250,000."

"$250,000? I can't do that!"

"I'm hanging up now...I'm almost ready to hang up. I really wanted to shoot that sonofabitch of yours anyway."

"Wait! Wait! I'll do it!"

"Little Bobby, there's hope for you after all. What a surprise. Now listen and write. I want the $250,000 in $50 and $20 bills. Don't try to get smart and mark the bills. Take my word for it—I'm an expert in the field. If I see they are all new bills so it would be very easy for you to write down the serial numbers, I'll burn all the bills and kill Craig before Saturday. Do we understand each other?"

"Yes, sir."

"This time I want the money in a red, white and blue, U. S. Post Office Priority Mailer, the rectangular, three-inches thick variety. Address it to yourself. Like last time, if you receive the package back at home, consider Craig dead. Remember that! When you have the money ready, instruct Craig to take the road to Hogback. Does Craig know where Hogback is?"

"Every one in Blue Ridge knows where Hogback is."

"Good. Tell Craig to drive out on the ridge until he comes to the first mailbox that can't be seen from the owner's house. Have him put the package near the box, on the ground, and raise the flag. I want him to place the package near the box no earlier than 10:00 Thursday morning. He then must return to the city jail before noon and stay there. If he isn't there to answer the phone, kiss him goodbye. Any questions?"

"No."

"Good, then tell me what you're going to do."

"I'm going to get $250,000 in old bills, $50 and $20 bills, put them in a self-addressed red, white and blue U. S. Post Office Mailer, the huge box variety. Craig will put the box right near the mail box on Hogback and answer the phone at the jail at noon on Thursday."

"Perfect. If Craig completes his job well, expect someone between 5:00 and 5:30 p.m. on Friday evening at your front door. This will be our last contact. Any questions?"

"Why are you doing this to me?"

"Why did you walk all over the people in Blue Ridge?" He hung up, immediately.

The next morning he noticed all the windows were closed at Mr. Bob's house. It was time to let Mike and Mother know he was leaving.

"Mike, I talked to Ron Creel. He's ready to start work."

"When are you leaving?"

"I have a ticket for Thursday morning."

"So soon?"

"The sooner I get there the sooner I can get back."

"That sounds good."

39

The Scoutmaster

"Mike where do you want me to leave the apartment key?"

"Just keep it. You'll be back soon."

"What if you need to get inside for something?"

"I don't know why I would, but if it will make you happy just stick it on top of the door frame, in the middle."

"I'll do that, sir."

"I guess you'll need your pay tomorrow?"

"Yeah, I will. Thanks."

Wednesday morning Mike announced they wanted to treat him to lunch. He agreed because he wanted so much for the Barkleys to remember him as a family member. When they finished lunch, Mrs. McKinney brought out a cake with one candle on it. Written on the top of the cake was *Jim, Hurry Back*. It hit him so hard he almost announced it was all a joke and he was staying. However, he knew his plan was in motion and couldn't be stopped. He only needed the help of one other person and that would be taken care of today.

When they departed the café he felt like he was leaving his family, walking out on the only mother and father he ever knew. He hadn't felt this depressed when the authorities took him off to jail. As they walked south on Main Street, he stopped in front of Mull Department Store.

"I hope you don't mind, but I need to get a few clothes for the trip. I shouldn't be more than, oh, five minutes, tops."

"Son, take your time. You've earned it."

"Thank you, sir."

As he entered the store a young man asked, "Can I help you?"

"Yes, I need a little bit of information. I see you sell Boy Scout equipment. You wouldn't know who the Scoutmaster in Blue Ridge is, would you?"

"Yep. That would be Jack Campbell. Are you looking to be an assistant scoutmaster?"

"Yes, I am. How did you know?"

"Just a guess. You are too old to be a scout," he said laughing.

"Do you know how I can get in touch with him?"

"Let me see. I think I have one of his cards. He's an insurance agent— Here it is. I'd call him at the office if I were you. I'm sure he could use the help."

"Thanks for your help."

"Your welcome and good luck on the scout thing."

He walked up the street and, seeing that no one was near the pay phone, he thought he should probably call Mr. Campbell now.

He dialed the number on the card. As it rang, he put his handkerchief over the mouthpiece as he always did. This time he wanted to be perceived as a female if possible.

"Is this Mr. Campbell?"

"Yes, ma'am. This is Jack Campbell. How can I help you?"

"I'm Mr. Bob's CPA. He wanted me to find out if he makes a donation to the Scouts will you provide him a receipt for tax purposes."

"Yes ma'am. I surely can."

"That's great. Mr. Bob would like to donate $2,000 to the Scouts."

"That would be wonderful. We'll be able to send most of our Scouts to summer camp on that amount. Could I pick up the check?"

"Yes, sir. If you'll," Jim coughed loudly, "excuse me."

"Ma'am, you need to take care of your cold."

"I know. It's all I can do to talk."

"I thought you sounded like you were sick. You were saying Mr. Bob would let me pick up the check."

"Yes, Mr. Campbell. He will. You do know how particular Mr. Bob is, don't you?"

"Yes, ma'am. I've heard."

"He would like for you to come to his house at 5:15 p.m., Friday evening. Can you do that?"

"I'll be there."

"Let me caution you. You can be five minutes early but you cannot be a minute late. Do you understand?"

"Yes, ma'am, I do. I'll be there on time and thank you for suggesting the Scouts."

"Why do you think it was me?"

"Because Mr. Bob once explained to me I was wasting my time with those delinquents and he wouldn't support them."

"I did inform him he needed another deduction. Mr. Bob is more motivated by money than anything."

"I know, the whole town knows. Thanks for thinking of the Scouts. I'll be there on time."

Walking back to the post office, Jim wished there was a real check in the wings for Mr. Campbell who seemed like a nice guy. Some things in life just aren't fair.

40
Dress Rehearsal

JIM SAID GOODBYE TO THE Barkleys that evening. Mother gave him a big hug and said, "You hurry home now! You don't come back and I'll go lookin' for you."

He didn't expect so much emotion from Mike. Tears came to his eyes and for a few moments he couldn't talk. Jim was moved by the big man's emotional state and finally Mike was able to say, "Hurry back," as he walked away. Jim didn't look back as he walked up the stairs to the apartment. As the door closed he checked the refrigerator and cupboard for food. For the next two days he must remain hidden from the Barkleys, as they expected him to leave on the Thursday morning bus and he couldn't afford for them to think otherwise.

Thursday he slept late, made coffee and ate doughnuts for breakfast and waited until the Barkleys left for lunch before he took a shower. He dressed and left the apartment by the rear path and stayed on the north side of town until they would go home in the late afternoon.

As 4:30 p.m. approached, he found a location where he could see them depart the post office. As soon as they were gone he moved to the loading ramp at the back of the post office and knew it was time for Joe O'Neal to return from delivering mail to Route 1 customers.

As Joe drove up, he jumped to his feet. Joe, surprised to see him, asked, "What's up?"

"Hi, Joe. I wanted to ask you a question."

"Shoot!"

"Mike was talking to me about taking the postal test. Before I did I thought I would talk to some of you old employees that have done it a while."

"Go ahead and say old timers!"

"No disrespect. Is it a good career?"

"I've been doing it for 30 years and I wouldn't want to do anything else."

"That's what I wanted to hear. Can I help you carry some of that stuff in?"

"That would be great."

He quickly grabbed Joe's mail tray, walked to the rear door and visually checked the contents along the way. It was outgoing mail Joe had picked up on his route, the right outgoing mail because as he entered the post office and tossed the contents in the air some he dislodged the letters in the tray just enough to see what he was looking for then sat the tray on the separating table.

Before Joe got inside, Jim sat the tray on the counter, took out the priority mailer box then quickly took off his jacket carefully wrapped the jacket around the box and placed it on a nearby chair. He then went outside and helped Joe finish unloading the truck.

"Thanks, Joe, for the information. I think this could be a career I could like."

"It is for me. Thanks for the help."

He was getting hungry but couldn't go out to eat. The risk of being seen by someone he knew was too great. He fixed a makeshift sandwich and a big salad with everything that was left in the fridge. He even found some of Mother's turkey and stuffing. At first he started to eat it then thought that it might be bad. He knew this was no time to get food poisoning.

He finally got around to checking the contents of the priority mailer box and was pleasantly surprised to find that Mr. Bob had followed his instructions to the letter. Most of the bills were $50s and they all looked used and unmarked. Inside was a note:

Here is your blood money. Now return Billy Bob's notebook.
Bob Foster

Still trying to get in the last word, huh asshole? Good try, but no way, Jim thought. That night he hung the extra blanket he had hoping it would help to cover the sound of the coming rifle shot. He placed the rifle on the shooting bench and began to scope the house. Then without warning the front door opened and there stood Craig. He quickly put the crosshairs on his chest. The sheriff's badge shined from the outside light. Jim centered the crosshairs on the sheriff's star. If the weapon had not been empty he could've completed his mission right then. As tempting as it was, he didn't do more than line up his scope. His escape plan would only work tomorrow—not tonight. He felt like he had just had a dress rehearsal for the shot he would make the next evening. When Craig answered the door, and he knew Craig would, he would make the shot. Now all that was left to do was wait, relish in a plan well thought out and keep out of sight.

41
The Shot

FRIDAY WAS AN ESPECIALLY LONG day, and filled with a great deal of anticipation. Jim woke at 5:00 a.m. and no matter how he tried couldn't get back to sleep.

He dry fired the mission three times during the morning and at noon began to pack his two bags for the trip. When that was complete, he decided Peggy might think it strange if he took everything he owned. After giving it some thought, he decided he'd only take one bag. He could always buy what he needed in California. He put everything else in the chest of drawers and even put some dirty clothes in the hamper Mother had provided.

He looked at the footlocker that the blankets had been in and decided he must repack the blankets before he left.

It was now 4:30 p.m. He went to the closet, but stopped. All at once his mouth was dry. He needed a drink first. After a long drink he climbed to the attic and prepared for the shot. At first he was a little hesitant but remembered the letter he had read about how Craig had taken advantage of a friendship by raping the friend's wife. As if that wasn't enough, he used his position in the community to legally kill a young father. *The prick is toast,* Jim thought. He further reflected on how a father and son had taken advantage of their position in the community... All these memories came rushing back at him as his anger rose. He was ready. It was time the Foster's tasted real sorrow—cold revenge for a life of abuse to others.

It was 5:10 p.m. when he saw Mr. Campbell walking up the long walkway to the house. He put the scope on the front door and took the rifle off of safety. As soon as he saw Craig, he would take a long breath, let it out and then squeeze the trigger. He was ready.

He held his position, trying to stay relaxed. Suddenly with his free eye, he saw movement. He looked over the scope and there was Craig coming around the house on the south side. He moved back to the scope and adjusted his aim to the left. He was looking for the badge on Craig's chest. It quickly appeared in the scope.

Holding his crosshairs on the target, he let out his breath and slowly squeezed the trigger. It was a surprise when the rifle exploded. Holding his aim he thought he saw the bullet strike just below the badge. The impact of the rifle bullet twisted Craig around.

Satisfied he'd made the shot, he removed the empty shell and the unused second round.

Now he had a lot of work to do and less than two hours to complete it.

First he raised the blanket near the ceiling vent and quickly replaced the missing louver then covered it with the blanket so no one could see the light. He then took down all the other blankets, unrolled the blanket off the one by one's, removing all the nails. He dropped them to the closet floor. He placed the pillowcase full of dirt in a paper bag he had selected just for this purpose.

Dropping the blankets to the closet floor, he climbed down then quickly folded the blankets and put them in the footlocker. He took the one by one and the paper bag out to the garden and stood the sticks in the corner next to the shed then emptied the dirt from the pillowcase. Even by turning it inside out he could not get all of the dirt out and decided he would take it with him and throw it away later.

He went back to the attic with his scissors and cut a two-foot strip off the blanket that covered the ceiling vent. Using the strip of blanket he wrapped his rifle and scope. He found some old shoestrings to tie it securely and then carried it downstairs and placed it next to his one suitcase.

Looking around, he took a big breath and decided he was done. Only the small piece of blanket was left upstairs. Taking his flashlight to the attic he turned off the ceiling lights. Once the lights were off he slowly made his way to the vent, lowering the blanket to see the activity. It was amazing that in only a few minutes there must have been at least twenty people show up out of nowhere.

He looked for Mr. Campbell and finally located him. It seemed like he was lowering someone to the ground. Others were pointing to the woods. So far he saw no police.

He removed the last blanket. As he walked back to the ceiling ladder he checked the area. It was a good thing because somehow he had dropped the empty shell. He placed it in his pocket.

Wanting to leave as soon as possible, he took one last look around the apartment. He placed his one bag and the blanket-wrapped rifle outside, closed and locked the door doing as Mike had instructed and placed the key on top of the doorframe. Carrying the bag, rifle and remaining piece of blanket, he went to the front of the post office. He sat the bag and rifle down and then walked to the rear of the post office and placed the piece of blanket in a box that someone had put in the trashcan.

Going around the post office he could see the crowd had grown. He now saw Dr. Burns running across the lawn. Two Georgia State Troopers came to meet the doctor. He wanted to leave in the worst possible way now and picked up the bag and rifle carrying it across the street to wait where Peggy always parked. He sat them behind a small bush and sat down to wait.

42

Peggy's Home

TRUE TO HER WORD, AT 7:30 p.m. Peggy turned into the parking lot. As she backed the Buick into her normal spot, he surprised her by opening her door. She jumped and scolded, "You scared me half to death!"

Jim, in a hurry, said, "I'm sorry. Give me your keys and I'll put my things in your trunk. Then we can get on our way."

Handing him the keys she asked, "What's the big rush?"

"This is our last night for a while and I don't want to waste it."

"Oh, if that's the case, hurry!"

He opened the trunk and placed the bag in first. He felt around for a place he could use to hide the rifle. The mat was loose next to the back seat. He pulled it back and placed the rifle up against the seat then replaced the mat. By pushing the blanket down behind the mat no one would ever see it without searching and there was no reason anyone would.

He closed the trunk, walked around and got in on the passenger side. He handed her the keys and said, "Let's go see what your bed is like."

"Now who's saying what's on their mind?"

"I had a good teacher."

As Peggy pulled out, she saw the crowd milling about at Mr. Bob's house.

"What's happening over there?"

"Who knows... I'm not sure, but I think some kids sent off a smoke bomb."

"It's what the bastard deserves," she muttered as she made a right turn to leave town. Not wanting to be seen with Peggy, he laid his head in her lap.

"What are you doing?"

"You keep telling me women can do two things at one time. I'm going to see."

"What's my Shy Guy up to?"

"I'm going to do a girdle check."

"No need. I didn't wear one."

"Then I'll do a panty check."

"No need, I'm wearing panties."

"Will you quit being so helpful? How am I ever going to touch you when you keep giving the answers?"

"Sorry. I thought I was helping. Is there some other check you can do? I'll try not to give the answer."

"Well, I know you have on a bra. I could check to see if your nipples are hard."

"What do you think?"

"You're telling me again."

"Sorry, it's just the teacher-in-control thing."

"Then I've one last check."

"What's that?"

"Are your panties wet yet?"

Peggy smiled.

"What are you smiling about?"

"I'm smiling because I don't know and I really want you to check."

He raised his head and asked, "You're not going to wreck, are you?"

"No! I can drive this route with my eyes closed."

"Where are we?"

"We just passed Cherry Log."

He began his slow trip up the inside of her leg. Each time he would move closer to her panties, she would let out a little gasp. When he was almost there she shifted her legs apart so he could make a better check. As she kept spreading her legs, her foot came off the gas peddle. The car quickly slowed. He sat up, "Ah ha! Can do two things at one time can you?" They laughed.

"Well, are they wet?"

"Ah, not sure. I'll wait until we are safely inside your house. How much farther is it?"

"Only twenty minutes."

The night went all too quickly. He was awakened at 6:00 a.m. with Peggy kissing his chest. He moaned, "You better watch that. You could get raped or something."

"Why do you think I'm doing it? I want the or something."

He rolled her over and forced himself to make slow, easy love. All was great until Peggy exploded with an orgasm of her own. Shortly it was over for him also.

They lay with Jim still on top trying to get his breath back. He began to roll off her, but Peggy stopped him.

"No. I want to remember this feeling. It will be a couple of months before I can feel it again."

He was speechless. Was it really true?

They took a shower and dressed. Peggy suggested breakfast at Howard Johnson's. After eating, they walked back to the car where Jim got in on the passenger side. Peggy walked to the driver's side and opened the door but just stood there for a moment. Jim looked at her wondering what was keeping her. She looked around the parking lot to see if anyone could see them. Satisfied the answer was no, she smiled, getting his attention, pulled her dress above her waist. She was wearing nothing underneath. He blushed as he normally did. Peggy smiled, "I just want you to know what's waiting for you, so hurry home."

She dropped the dress and climbed in the car.

43

The Airport

T HEY TALKED ALL THE WAY to the airport, neither one saying anything of importance. As they approached the airlines outside check-in, Jim just said, "Drop me off at the curb. It's hard enough to leave as it is."

"Okay, if you'll finish your work in Texas as soon as possible and hurry home."

"I promise."

Retrieving his bag from the trunk, he made a quick check on the rifle. It was still well covered and he closed the trunk. He waved as Peggy drove away. It then hit him he was truly in love with her. He slowly approached the Delta counter where the older woman at the desk asked, "Where to today, sir?"

"California."

"San Diego, Los Angeles or San Francisco?"

"Which one leaves next?"

"That would be Flight 192 to Los Angeles. It has one stop over in Dallas."

"No direct flights?"

"That's correct, sir. The San Francisco flight is direct and it leaves at noon."

"I'll take it then."

"How will you pay, sir?"

"Cash, I think. How much is it?"

"One way, or round trip?"

"One way."

"Five hundred and forty dollars."

"I'll pay cash."

That night was Jim's first to see the sun set on the Pacific Ocean.

44

San Francisco

SAN FRANCISCO WAS BEAUTIFUL ANY time of year but in perfect weather conditions it was absolutely breathtaking. But he couldn't enjoy it because of worrying about the obvious. He wasn't worried about the events in Blue Ridge because from all appearances things had gone as planned. What he could not stop worrying about was the cash he had hidden in the lining of his coat. When he combined the $250,000 he had received from Mr. Bob with the money he still had from his other jobs it came to more than $700,000. Now that was a coat worth dying for. He felt all he could do was stay in his room until Monday morning when the banks opened.

As he got into a taxi, he said, "Take me to the nicest hotel in town!" Clearly, he knew what he was doing and felt the more expensive hotel would lessen his chances of being mugged.

He made a game of it at the check-in counter. " I asked the taxi driver to take me to the best hotel in town. Is this it?"

"Yes, sir, and has been for years."

"The Mark Hopkins. Sounds classy. Do you have a room I can rent?"

"Do you want a room or a suite?"

"Ma'am, let me be honest. I have $1200 and plan to spend it on a room. It was a gift but I must blow it all at once on something I want. What I want is the best room I can get until Wednesday. Can you help me?"

"Indeed, sir. I'll be glad to. I'll give you a room that we set aside for a special guest. The person who had it reserved is out of the country at the moment and it's empty. I'll only change you $1100 until noon on Wednesday."

"Ma'am, you've made a country boy real happy. Please keep the other hundred for being so nice."

"Thank you, sir. If you need anything else just let me know. My name is Lisa Small."

She handed him her card. Even with the friendly reception he received from the hotel staff he felt the safest choice was to use room service for his meals and just watch TV. How could he go wrong? He decided this was a classy hotel because his room had a color TV in the bathroom. He wondered how long it would take for the motels and hotels in Georgia to get color television.

After spending all weekend alone he began to think about his future. His revenge drive was over. He could see other directions on the horizon for his life now. He could've stopped earlier had Craig not killed Sam McGill. That said, he didn't regret killing Craig, but it did force him to leave Peggy.

Starting Monday he determined to make a new life for himself. Maybe, just maybe, this new life would cross Peggy's. He wondered if she knew he was nothing more than a delinquent when young and had spent his latter teen years in jail if she would still think he was so special. Maybe one day he would find out, one day soon.

Monday morning he began walking the streets of San Francisco. He had to admit this city by the sea had a special charm, trolley cars the opera, the whole ten yards. As a young man in Washington, Georgia, he'd never dreamed he would ever ride cable cars. But now his first mission was to find the right bank.

He finally found one he thought would serve the purpose. When he entered, he asked the guard at the door who he needed to see to get a safety deposit box.

"That would be Jane Woodall, a class act if I say so myself."

Thanking him, Jim approached her desk.

"The gentleman at the door said you were the nicest lady here and you'd take good care of me."

She blushed, "Uncle Jim says that about every woman in this bank."

"He sounded sincere to me."

"Sir, how can I help?"

"Ma'am, I need a safety deposit box."

"Do you have an account with us?"

"No, ma'am, just arrived this weekend. I hadn't been here two hours when someone stole my wallet. Before I lose any other paperwork, I want to put them in a safe place." Jim patted the new briefcase he had just purchased.

"Well, sir, we usually require our customers to open an account first."

"That will be okay with me but the only ID I have is my social security number."

"I think we can make an exception in your case. Let me get some information and I'll take it to our manager. What is your home address?"

"I'm living at the Mark Hopkins."

"On Nob Hill?"

"I'm not sure if that's right or not, as I just arrived. Here is their business card. If it makes you feel better and will speed up the process, why don't you call them and verify that Jim Coleman is a guest?"

"If you don't mind, sir. Please excuse me." She was gone for about ten minutes and then returned with two cards in her hand.

"Mr. Coleman, I just need your signature on these cards. What size box do you need?"

"A big one. I have some deeds and other legal papers."

She pointed out the size of the three samples on a nearby desk. He took the middle one.

"How much is that one?"

"It'll be $25 every six months."

"Can I pay a year in advance?"

"I was going to suggest that because you don't currently have an account with us."

"That will change when I get my wallet back."

"Mr. Coleman, if you will follow me I'll take you to your box."

He followed her into a separate area filled with wall-to-wall boxes. She removed the one with his number on it and placed it in front of him in a separate, private area. When he was alone he ripped the lining from his coat and started putting the money in the safety deposit box. He kept $500 for spending money.

Now that the money was in a safe place, he began to relax and enjoy the sites. He rode the cable car and walked to Fisherman's Wharf for a good crab/shrimp dinner at the Franciscan, plenty of sourdough bread, famous the world over. After finishing off a big serving of crabs he began to notice a few help-wanted signs. The first two he inquired about wanted an experienced person. The third didn't mind that he didn't have experience as the job was for a part-time dishwasher. He took the job.

He approached one of the other employees in the kitchen to find a place to live. The fellow worker suggested Chinatown, stating the rooms could be rented cheaply and it was easy to catch a cable car to work. He thanked the worker for his help. Before leaving he checked with his new boss to see what time he needed to start work. Information in hand, he found a newsstand that had city maps for sale.

When he returned to the hotel he fell across the bed and began to review the day. The money was safe and he had a part-time job and a place to live. All in all, it had been a very productive day. He was beginning to feel good about the new life he was starting for himself and began to think about his next move. Then he had an inspiration—time to get a driver's license. Of course he needed to learn to drive first, and hadn't driven since Sonny let him drive his new T-Bird.

He pulled out the telephone book located in the nightstand next to the bed. He quickly located several driver schools. His eye went to one school that guaranteed you would get your California driver's license or your money back. He wasn't sure what kind of paperwork issues were ahead of him, but he felt this was a school that knew how to cut red tape.

He called the driving school and explained he had just moved from Georgia. He asked if they could help. They assured him that he would be completely satisfied with their service. He made an appointment for the next day after work. Sorting things out in his head, he didn't really need to work, but only being a part-time employee meant he still had plenty of time to himself. This would give him an opportunity and the time to meet the right people. He could also ask for help and directions from his coworkers. It was possible many of the people he would work with were in the same state of life as he and were still looking for directions.

After a few months he knew twenty people by their first names, was the proud owner of a California driver's license and had taken his first course at the local community college. He was terrified at first that with only a GED he could never go to college. He'd discovered that a few of the people he worked with only had GEDs. In fact, one of them had been in community college for two years and had just been accepted at UCLA for the fall.

The old adage was certainly true—the hardest step of a rewarding journey was the first one. That he had taken—

45

A Surprise

LIFE CONTINUED TO GET BETTER in California. Too, he was falling in love with San Francisco, if one could possibly fall in love with a city. Doing something about his education made him realize how important self-esteem was to any young man. Perhaps he was worthy of a life with Peggy after all. He just wished he could have Peggy with him but that would mean a whole lot of explaining and he wasn't at the bridge just yet. He began to think maybe he could go back to Georgia and continue his education there. He then remembered the newsstand where he found the city maps his second day in San Francisco had also carried the *Atlanta Journal* He slipped on his jacket and caught a cable car to get one. He was excited just thinking about returning to Georgia, so much so he could hardly stand it. It was the first week in June and late spring was always so beautiful in the mountains.

At the newsstand, he couldn't find the Atlanta paper. Disappointed, he asked the attendant if they had a copy.

"Yeah, look under the *Wall Street Journal.*"

He moved the stack of papers and sure enough there was what he was looking for. He paid the attendant and began the trek back to his room. He planed to read it from cover to cover. There must be as many opportunities in Atlanta as there were in San Francisco.

As soon as he returned to the room he reordered his thinking and got himself a beer and began to read. He had not noticed before that a picture of a woman took up one-fourth of the front page. The headlines read: *Pregnant Woman To Be Put On Death Row...*

Miss Margaret Taylor was convicted for the first-degree murders of her father and brother. The shooting took place on the lawn of the family home in Blue Ridge, Georgia. Witness testimony placed her at the scene on the night of the murders. The disclosure at the trial that police had recovered the murder weapon and spent shells inside the car of the accused assured the prosecution of a quick victory. Jurors returned with a guilty verdict after only thirty minutes of deliberation.

Jim stopped reading. He was in shock. What had he done? Could this be his Peggy he was reading about? It couldn't be. Could it? The paper said she was the daughter and sister. Then a cold chill came over him. She's pregnant. Could it be his child?

He was paralyzed for a moment. He could only look at the picture and read the headline. He knew he had to do something, but he had no clue what it should be. He tried to relax and get control of himself. The more he thought of the situation he had created, the more he felt panic taking control.

He had once read that if you are in a panic situation just do something, even if it amounts to just peeing in your pants. Well, he wasn't going to do that, but he did start making a list. The more he wrote the more rational he found himself becoming. He tried to stay away from areas that he couldn't control. The area that caused him the most feelings of panic was when he thought of Peggy. How was he going to fix this mess?

He made a mental note that he would list the things he could control. He knew he must return to Blue Ridge. That was a given. What needed to be done before he left? As his list grew, the more control he had. He actually began to relax. One thing at a time, one day at a time and one solution at a time was what he kept repeating in his head.

46
Return to Blue Ridge

T HE PLANE RIDE TO ATLANTA seemed so much longer than when he flew to California. He had much time to think about Peggy and the mess he'd created. She was innocent and he might be the only person on earth who knew that. Then he locked his thoughts on Peggy being pregnant and that made it even worse. He had mixed emotions about a baby. Having a baby with Peggy would be the most wonderful thing in the world, but Peggy being in jail made it an impossible situation.

On the plane he just had his thoughts. When the bus passed through Jasper the scenery began to remind him of the wonderful time he had spent with Peggy, the happiest times of his life. He was almost ready to explode when the bus stopped in front of the Blue Ridge station.

As he stepped off the bus he remembered it was almost one year to the day since he had first stepped onto this sidewalk. At that time he had arrived with pure vengeance in his heart. This time his heart was full of desperation. He began his walk to the post office. Each step increased his apprehension. What would the Barkleys do? Would they still feel the same about him or would they want nothing to do with him? If they refused to even talk with him, he would understand beyond words.

He was surprised to see the same little group sitting near the post office. It looked like he had only been gone a couple of days instead of months. He still approached the lobby slowly. Then he heard Mike's booming voice call out, "Mother! Look who's home. It's Jim!"

They both almost attacked him with hugs and kisses. Mother made him feel like he was a war hero that had been missing for years. She began to talk a mile-a-minute. She had cleaned his apartment, washed all his clothes and his bed linens, waiting every day for his return. They had even added a TV to the room while he was gone. He had a sickening feeling in his stomach. Not only had he destroyed Peggy's life, he was doing even worse to the Barkleys. They had lost their Michael to the Vietnam War and now Mother refused to accept the loss of Jim. He thought if he had stayed in California how many more months would Mother have lasted? All at once he was ashamed of how selfish he had become. He made a pledge that being selfish would never be part of his life again.

47

Reviewing the Past

THE BARKLEYS INSISTED HE COME with them for supper. Jim was surprised.

"I thought you ate out."

Mike smiled, "Only on weekends. Mother now likes fixing supper for us. It's made us feel more like a family again. Jim, we'd like you to feel as if you are part of our family."

"I would love that, but first I need to let you know more about me before you decide to welcome me with open arms."

That night after Mother cleared the table and cut them each a piece of apple pie for dessert he decided it was time to bring the Barkleys into his secret world.

"Mike, I'd like to talk to you about something very serious, like big time."

Mother spoke first, "Jim, please tell us. You seem to be carrying a big load. Maybe we can help."

"I'm not sure you will think much of me when I tell you everything."

"Let us be the judge of that."

"My real name is Coleman, not Cole. I didn't tell you because I spent half of my teen years in a detention center."

"We suspected something like that."

"You never let on."

"Mother and I try to judge people by what they do now, not by what they may have done in the past. We knew you would tell us someday if we needed to know."

"Thank you, sir. You have treated me better than my own parents. That's the reason I want you to know everything. I was a real troublemaker when I was young. When the son of our town leader got into trouble, my father and he struck a deal where I would accept the punishment. My father was a drunk and it's a long story, but the end result was I went to jail. While there, the same son raped my sister. She committed suicide and my mom died shortly after that."

Mother, "My God! How awful. No wonder you didn't want to be around people."

"Did you confront the son when you got out? Is that it?" Mike said.

"No, sir. I planned to but both father and son were killed in a car accident six months before my release. I wanted you to know the complete story so you would understand why I only have a GED and not a high school diploma. Also, and more important, I need to help Peggy and I'm sure my past will come out. I didn't want you to find out that way. You have both been too good to me."

"We understand. We also wondered when you would bring Peggy up. We know her as Margaret. That's why we didn't recognize her as your Peggy."

"Do you know why she changed her name?"

"I'm not sure, but something happened her last year in college. We had heard she would start teaching at West Fannin High School in the fall after graduating, but that didn't happen. The prosecutor brought out that Peggy's roommate had committed suicide. He went on to say Peggy blamed her brother and when her father took Craig's side Peggy rebelled and changed her name."

"Mike, why would they bring all that up in court?"

"Remember before you left to help your friend, Craig shot and killed Sam McGill?"

"Yes, sir."

"Well, Sue, Sam's wife, was Peggy's roommate for a year. The prosecutor built his case based on Peggy's losing control when she heard what Craig did."

"The newspaper said she killed her father also. When did that happen?"

"You don't know?"

"Know what?"

"Mr. Bob was killed with the same bullet that killed Craig."

"How could that be?" The question just flew out of his mouth. This news was just too much for him. The situation was more complicated than he had first thought. Mike tried to answer his question but Jim wasn't really listening. Something about Mr. Bob being behind Craig when he was shot. Jim did hear him say that they were shot from the woods behind Mr. Bob's house. He had depended on a sloppy investigation of Craig's death. However, he did not want the blame to be placed on an innocent person—especially Peggy. He was extremely confused with this new information. He tried to compose himself. He felt the Barkleys knew enough about him already. He needed some time to himself to work out this mess. He also needed much more information but did not want to get it from the Barkleys. Nick was the solution. His law background could help him turn this mess around.

"Mother, thanks for the best meal I have ever had."

"You're welcome, I love to cook for men that eat."

"Mike, I would like my old job back if that is possible. However, I need a few days before I start. I would like to visit Peggy if I could."

"We understand. You just let us know when you are ready to work."

"Thank you, sir. Do you know where they took Peggy after the trial?"

"They didn't take her any where. She is still in the county jail behind the courthouse."

"Really? I would have thought they would take her to Atlanta."

"Normally, yes, but her being pregnant and all changed everything. She is to remain here until she has the baby."

"Then what?"

"Atlanta."

"What about the baby?"

"Judge Foster is Peggy's nearest relative. I've heard he and his wife are going to adopt the baby."

"Can they do that?"

"Son, I think it's already done."

He was sick to his stomach. More horrible news came at him by the ton. What should he do? What could he do? The Barkley's saw the pain on his face. They looked at each other and Mother whispered to Mike, "Take him home, that's enough bad news for tonight. I can't stand to watch him suffer."

Mike agreed. "Jim, let me drive you back to the apartment." Almost in a trance, he nodded "Thanks!"

48
Getting Settled

HE KNEW THE FIRST THING he needed to do was get his money in a safe place, having drawn everything out of the bank in San Francisco before boarding the aircraft for Atlanta. He still had over $700,000—too much to put in his hiding place under the bed. Putting all the money in his briefcase, he decided to eat breakfast at the café while waiting for the bank to open. Mrs. McKinney saw him come through the door.

"Welcome back, stranger. You know the Barkleys surely did miss you, son!"

"I missed them, too."

"It's nice to see you. What can I get you?"

"A couple of eggs, bacon and coffee, please."

"Comin' right up."

He drank his coffee while listening to the conversations of the other customers. He realized the topics were the same ones he had listened to last fall. It looks like the removal of two snakes had no effect on this town. He had erased Billy Bob and Craig for pure revenge and thought the town would have gotten better somehow. Instead it looked like business as usual.

He was the first bank customer and asked whom to see to open a savings account. The clerk pointed to a neatly dressed, middle age woman saying, "Mrs. White, can help you."

Thanking her, he approached the desk. "I need to open two accounts and get a safety deposit box."

"Sir, take a seat. I need a little information."

The whole process was so much easier than he'd thought. In less than thirty minutes he had a safety deposit box, a checking and a savings account. As he walked out the door, he realized he was now officially a resident of Blue Ridge, Georgia—a resident who had created a mess only God could fix.

It was time to see Nick. If anyone could come up with a plan, it was Nick. The walk to the supper club was like coming home. He felt more at home here than he did in Washington, Georgia, where he was born and reared. He wondered why that was. He'd only lived in Blue Ridge for six months, but those six months were filled with love and happiness. With Nick's help, maybe he could recapture all that, somehow, some way.

As he walked into the parking lot of the supper club, Nick came out with a bag of trash. Nick saw him, "Where in the hell have you been, boy? Your girlfriend has gotten herself in a peck of trouble."

"I know. That's why I'm here. What can we do to get her out?"

"I think maybe it's too late for that."

"It can't be. She's innocent."

"You and I know that, but the jury said otherwise."

"I can't believe everyone on the jury felt that way."

" I was there. They polled the jury. Every one of them said guilty."

"Nick, help me out here. Tell me everything you know about the case."

"I'll try. Here it is... She was seen leaving town shortly after Craig and Mr. Bob were both shot. Two more people testified they saw her leaving town in a hurry. One of the witnesses, Tad Green, said he saw a man lying down in her front seat. At first they thought she had an accomplice. When they found the empty shell on her car's front seat, they found a fingerprint that didn't match Peggy's. Later they discovered that the deputy carrying the evidence dropped the envelope. The empty shell fell out and he just picked it up with his bare hand and put it back in the envelope. The other print was then smudged. They even talked about you as an accomplice until the bus driver told the GBI investigator that he had picked up five passengers on Thursday, the day before the killing. He verified a man fitting your description was one of the passengers."

"They sure were quick on going to trial."

"Remember, the county judge is Mr. Bob's sister's boy. He saw an opportunity to show off for the big boys in Atlanta. Everything was done in less than four months. They made it look like it was a simple family dispute that got out of control."

"Nick, why didn't you tell me that Peggy was Mr. Bob's daughter?"

"It wasn't any of my business. Would it have made any difference in the way you feel about her?"

"No, not how I feel. But perhaps it would have changed something."

"I'm sure Peggy would have gotten around to telling you sooner or later. Especially when she found out she was pregnant. Jim is that baby yours?"

"Absolutely. I know it's mine. Nick, what on earth am I going to do?"

"What do you want to do?"

"I need to see Peggy. Maybe then we'll know what to do. Do you think they'll let me see her?"

"I think this is a case of it's easier to get forgiveness than it is to get permission. I still have a lot of friends at the jail from when I was sheriff. Let's wait until after 5:00 o'clock and I'll see what I can do."

"Nick, I appreciate this so much."

"I just wish I could do more."

49

First Visit With Peggy

NICK AND JIM ARRIVED AT the county jail that was sullen, quiet and fairly empty. The guards were happy to see Nick. They all shook his hand and patted him on the back. Then they got to the important question. "To what do we owe the pleasure of your company, Nick?"

"My friend, Jim, would like to see his friend, Peggy Taylor."

"I'm not sure we can do that."

"Bob, let's keep it simple. He will be gone before you can find someone to give you permission. As I remember it, you didn't ask me for a lot of permission when I was sheriff."

"Got me there, Sheriff. I mean, Nick. Okay, come on back. I suppose I can give him thirty minutes."

"Sir, thank you so much."

Jim didn't know what to expect when he saw her, but was surprised to see the big smile on her face. "Oh, darling. Jim, it's so wonderful to see you. I thought you'd forgotten the way home."

"Peggy you look so beautiful. I thought this mess would have changed you."

"I have changed. Didn't you notice? I'm pregnant."

"Still outspoken, I see."

"Don't you just love it?"

"I love you more than life itself."

"How do you feel about being a Daddy?"

"I would love it even more if you were out of here."

"Me, too, but we must play the hand that was dealt."

"We'll appeal this and get you out."

"My lawyer tells me I don't have enough of a reason to get an appeal."

"Is he a good lawyer?"

"The best I could afford."

"Do you need money?"

"Not now. Tell me why you took so long to come home."

"No real reason. I just got involved in learning to drive and continuing my education so I could come back and marry you."

"Is that a marriage proposal?"

"If you will, it is."

"It's about time you made an honest woman out of me."

"Are you serious?"

"I couldn't be any more serious. Our son needs a father."

"How do you know it's a son?"

"He kicks too hard to be a girl," smiled Peggy.

"Oh, sweetie. I have so many questions to ask and something I must tell you about me. First, my name is Jim Coleman, not Cole. I want our son to have a legal name."

"Are you going to tell me you are already married?"

"No. Absolutely not. I just want you."

"We can talk about these little stupid problems later. For now I need to know if we can really get married. Jim, I don't want our son to be raised by Judge Roy Bean."

"Me either. Roy Bean? Is that a joke?"

"What happened to your sense of humor?"

"I think I left it outside the jail."

The guard approached the cell, "You must leave now, the doctor is scheduled to arrive in ten minutes."

"Thanks for allowing us time to see each other."

"Anything for Nick."

"Peggy, I will take care of what we talked about. I promise."

"I love you, Jim"

"I love you too."

50

Planning A Wedding

AS NICK AND JIM WALKED to the car, Jim filled him in on what he wanted to do.

"If you two are serious about getting married then you better do it quickly before the word gets out that you're back."

"They wouldn't stop us, would they?"

"You never know, but I expect they'll try."

As Nick drove back to the supper club he announced, "Jimmy, my boy, I guess we're going to get you married. Are you up for it?"

"Would you help us?"

"Hey, what're friends for? First you'll need a marriage license. Leave that up to me. Next you'll need a preacher. Do you know one?"

"No, but I'll bet Mr. Barkley does."

"You're right and if he asked for you how could a good, God-fearing preacher refuse?"

"You mean the preacher could refuse to marry us?"

"Remember, you're in Blue Ridge and Peggy is a convicted murderer. What would his congregation think? They might just vote him out of the pulpit."

"I didn't think it was going to be so hard to do."

"Relax. Nothing worthwhile is ever easy. I'll pick you up at 9:00 a.m. and we can get the license situation out of the way. Before I get there, talk to the Barkleys and let them in on what's going down. Let them know you need a preacher ASAP. If I know them, getting a preacher will be the easy part."

"Nick, I know you are my friend, but doing all of this for me is more than a friend should have to do."

"Nonsense, my boy. This is exciting. I haven't felt this good since… What do you know? I haven't felt this good in my entire life! It just goes to show you when you do the right thing for the right reason it feels great. Now let's you and me go get a steak at Harry's."

"What about the supper club?"

"Tuesday is always slow. Maybe I will start a new routine. Tuesday will be steak night with friends!"

He had many questions to ask Nick, too many for the present evening and this just didn't feel to be the right time. Getting married seemed an almost impossible task by itself. He just took this opportunity to tell Nick about his childhood and his detention years. Nick also shared some of his past with him. It was as if the sharing cemented their friendship for life.

Nick dropped him off in front of the post office and waved good night.

Jim climbed the stairs and went straight to bed. He had a restful sleep, obviously well needed.

51
Getting the License

T HE NEXT MORNING HE AWOKE refreshed and ready to take on the world, hardly able to wait for the Barkleys to arrive. He met them at the door with a big smile.

"You ready to work so soon?" asked Mike.

"No, sir. I have a major favor to ask."

"What's that, son?"

"Would you be the best man at my wedding?"

Shocked, "Are you and Peggy getting married?"

"Yes, sir. If we can."

"When?"

"As soon as Nick and I can make the arrangements."

"Nick Turner is helping you?"

"Yes. Is that a problem?"

"Not really. If anyone in this county can get it done, he's your man. I'm just surprised he'd leave the supper club. He's been holed up in there like a hermit since he was defeated as sheriff years ago."

"That's a surprise. He took me to see Peggy last night and then we had steaks at Harry's."

"Well, I'll be... You must've changed him. We all thought he would just drink himself to death in that club, sort of disappear into a drinking glass. It's good to hear he's alive again."

"Mike, Nick suggested you might know a preacher that would marry us."

"I sure do! Reverend Harper. He was the minister at Barnes Chapel Church. Reverend Harper lost his only son in the great WW2. When he heard about our Michael, he came to see us. If it hadn't been for him, I don't know how we would have made it."

"Nick said the preacher might not want to marry us because of Peggy's being convicted."

"Don't you worry. Reverend Harper will do it because it's the right thing to do. When is this wedding going to take place?"

"If we can, I'd like to do it today."

"Today? Well, I guess, why not—"

"Yes. Nick thinks Judge Foster may try to stop it if we wait much longer."

"He's right! The Fosters already have plans for that baby. Your marriage could ruin them. I'll round up the Reverend. What time do you want him at the jail?"

"Let's all meet here at one o'clock and go together."

"If I can't find Reverend Harper, I'll find someone else, so don't you worry. Mike turned to his wife, "Mother, we're going to a wedding. Better go home and get dressed."

Shortly after that Nick drove up in front of the post office, walked to the sidewalk and up the short steps and opened the door. "I explained everything to Mike," Jim said. "He says Reverend Harper will marry us Mike will have the Reverend here at one o'clock. Do we need anything else?"

"Not really. We need the license though. Let's work on that now."

Nick was caught by the traffic light as he drove away from the post office. It was the first time Jim had the opportunity to see Mr. Bob's house. He looked across the lawn and to his surprise the house was gone. There was a large sign announcing it as the future home of the Fannin County Bank. Turning to Nick, "What happened to Mr. Bob's house?"

"Peggy didn't tell you?"

"No. What?"

"She sold the house and lot to the bank so she could pay her lawyer."

"How did she get it so quickly?"

"Mr. Bob had deeded it to her years ago, trying to buy her forgiveness. She had forgotten until Mr. Bob's lawyer reminded her. She sold the property to them under the condition that the house had to be destroyed in thirty days. The bank had a bulldozer there the next week. Who says things don't happen fast in Fannin County?"

Nick parked in front of the courthouse and turned to Jim and warned him to let him do all the talking. Nick was serious.

Jim smiled and said, "Okay. I wouldn't know what to say anyway."

As they walked into the clerk's office the lady recognized Nick with a big smile.

"Hey, sheriff. How're you doin'?"

"Great, Lisa, and how are you?"

"I'm fine."

"How's your father?"

"Wonderful."

"How old is he now?"

"Eighty-seven!"

"Eighty-seven? Does he still drive the tractor?"

"Oh, yeah. He's not that kind of eighty-seven just yet. He's afraid we might break it so only he drives it. Wait 'til I tell him I saw you today."

"Tell him I heard he was selling his corn by the gallon again."

"Now Sheriff, play fair... You know he quit making shine some twenty years ago!"

"Yeah, I know, but it will remind him of the good old times anyway."

"It will. You know you should go see him. He really respected you."

"I can't think of anyone I respect more than your father. I may just do that!"

"I know he would appreciate it. Do it for me. Now, how can I help you?"

"I need a special favor, Lisa, and I need for you to keep it a secret for a couple of days. You are to tell no one, and I mean no one."

"Sounds exciting. What is it?"

"Well, Jim here wants to get married and he needs a marriage license."

"That's easy. What's the big secret?"

"He going to marry Peggy Taylor."

"What!"

"Yes. He's the father of her baby and they want to make it legal. The reason we want you to keep it a secret is you know what these newspaper reporters will do with this type of news and if it gets to the Fosters even some other way—"

"Sheriff, I understand, I understand...but I will still need her signature."

"Could you let me take the form to her?"

"No, but if you and Jim will sit down over there while I take my coffee break we will finish the paperwork later." She smiled and winked as they took their seats. Twenty minutes later she returned.

"How was your coffee?"

"It was wonderful. She will make a beautiful bride. Mr. Coleman, will you please sign here? That will be $5, please."

"Lisa, may you be in heaven five minutes before the devil knows you're dead."

"Same to you, sheriff. Maybe ten minutes in your case."

"Thank you, ma'am," Jim said.

"You're welcome sir and take care of that baby of yours."

"I will," was his quick response.

On the way to the car, Jim thought, *How in the world am I going to care for a baby? I've got to get Peggy free even if it means going to jail myself.* Nick suggested they go see how the Barkleys were doing with Reverend Harper, lined up for 1:00 o'clock.

It was only 11:00 a.m. when they got back to the post office. As promised, Mike had a preacher. Looking at him, Jim was sure he was the preacher, an elderly man in a black suit holding a well-worn Bible in his right hand, just like he stepped out of the 1946 John Ford movie, *My Darling Clementine,* starring Henry Fonda. Mike spoke first, "Jim, this is Reverend Harper."

"Nice to meet you, sir."

"Nice to meet you, young man. Are you the one in the big hurry to get married?"

"Yes, sir, I am. I have the marriage license here."

"If you don't mind, give it to me and I will take care of getting them filed for you."

"Thank you, sir."

"Son, are you sure this is what you want to do?"

"With all my heart."

"Then let's get started."

Mike looked at Nick, "Do you think they will let us in the jail, now, I mean?'

"We won't know 'til we try," Nick said. "Who's going?"

"Me and the missus, Reverend Harper, you and Jim, I guess," replied Mike.

"Good. Jim, you ride with me. We'll see the rest of you in front of the jail."

52

Getting Married

NICK ASKED THE POLICEMAN ON jail duty if Sheriff Williams was there.

"Yes, sir. Who can I tell him is here?"

"Nick Turner."

"Sheriff Turner?"

"Long time ago, son. Too long—"

Sheriff Williams met Nick at the door. "Well, well. Look what the cat's dragged home. How are you Nick?"

"Fine, and you?"

"Okay, I guess. I didn't know how hard you had to work at this job or I wouldn't have run against you."

"Does keep you busy, doesn't it."

"Nick, what are you up to? I understand you never leave that hole you work in."

"No place to go and no need—until today."

"Meanin' what?"

"The truth is we want to get this boy married to Miss Peggy. However; I have too much respect for you to go behind your back."

"I appreciate that. What do you want me to do?"

"Just let Reverend Harper marry them here in the jail. But you need to know their marriage may make Judge Foster awfully mad."

"Nick, this is my jail. I'm an elected official just like he is. Let him be mad. I have a feeling his rooster-crowin' days are over."

"Then you'll do it?"

"Do it? I want to be one of the witnesses! I'll even sign on the marriage certificate! Follow me."

"Is it alright if Mr. and Mrs. Barkley join us?"

"Absolutely. Mike, Martha, excuse my manners. I didn't realize you were standing there. Please, join us?"

Mike shook his hand and said humbly, "We won't forget this sheriff."

"I'm depending on it!" he laughed.

They arrived in front of Peggy's cell to find her holding the bars. "What's going on?" she said.

Jim spoke first. "You said you would marry me and I'm going to make sure you don't back out."

Tears flooded her eyes and she choked with emotion, "I love you, Jim Coleman."

The sheriff asked Reverend Harper where he wanted to do the ceremony. "I guess Jim can just stand there next to her."

"No way!" announced the sheriff. "Tommy! Bring me the keys to this cell. I don't think escaping is quite on her mind right now. Let's move into the large room over there. Reverend Harper, they're all yours."

As a good Baptist minister, Reverend Harper felt he needed to preach a short sermon before he married them. It seemed acceptable to everyone as they quieted down to listen. Mr. and Mrs. Barkley stood hand in hand, both of them fighting back tears. They had come to love Jim and were overjoyed to participate in the wedding, though extremely emotional knowing that shortly it could end with Peggy's execution. Because of their own precious experiences of sharing a life with someone you loved, they could truly appreciate how special was the moment and event. It seemed everyone was holding his breath waiting to hear Reverend Harper begin. He spoke for several minutes and then said, "This is where I normally ask who gives the bride away."

Mike cleared his throat and said quickly, "I'd like that honor if it's okay with you Margaret."

Peggy began to cry and threw her arms around his neck whispering, "Why couldn't my father have been more like you?"

Mike quietly thanked her and held her until she got control of her emotions again. The rest of the service was absolutely beautiful but bittersweet, in light of an outcome no one wanted to talk about.

After giving them a few minutes, Sheriff Williams informed them they would all have to leave. Nick thanked him and said, "You know you will have a few rough days with the judge."

"I know, but it's been worth it." Seeing Jim leave with the others, he called out, "Jim, where are you going?"

"Sir?"

"You just got married, didn't you? We don't marry folks around here and then let them go separate."

"What do you mean?"

"It's not the Ritz, but you and your bride can have her room until five o'clock."

"Can you do that?"

"I just did. Tommy, if anyone, and I mean anyone, tries to bother these two before 5:00 you better look for another job. Do I make myself clear?"

"Yes, Sheriff."

"They WILL have their privacy," Tommy said.

Mrs. Barkley had turned around to catch the eye of Sheriff Williams. He smiled, "Martha, I used to be a romantic."

"You still are," was her quiet reply.

53
Married

ALONE IN HER CELL, JIM and Peggy sat on the edge of the bed.

"Let me hold you," begged Peggy.

For a long while they just stayed in each other's arms.

Then Jim whispered, "I have never made love to a pregnant woman before."

"Well, I have never been pregnant before, so we're even, sailor."

"I'm afraid I'll hurt you or the baby."

"Still my Shy Guy, huh? Just think of me as...as your fat sex goddess."

They took off their clothes and began to touch each other it was as if they were back in his apartment. The biggest and most terrible difference was the ghost in the room—death itself. It was so hard for them to touch and love each other with the fact that in a few months' Peggy could be put to death—and for a crime she had nothing to do with and was innocently innocent. In the past they had the feeling they could not get close enough with their bodies because of love and lust. Now it was different. The feeling was even stronger because this could be the last time they would ever achieve this intimacy. They prolonged the inevitable as long as possible. Peggy was the first to succumb to her passion. It first started with her neck turning blood red, and then she became very rigid, screaming into his ear, "I'm coming, baby. Let go, come with me."

With those pleading words, he exploded. Peggy began to laugh out loud.

"I've never had that effect on you before," he said.

"I never had a football player inside of me before. He was trying to kick the field goal."

"Is he okay?"

"Oh, yes. And me, too, if you want to know."

"Oh, Peggy. You know what I mean."

"You're always going to be my Shy Guy, aren't you?"

"I guess, as long as you want me anyway."

54

Complete Truth

AFTER AN HOUR OF TOUCHING and simply appreciating each other beyond words Peggy finally broke the silence. "Are you the one who shot Craig?"

Jim was shocked and speechless.

"It won't make any difference about how I feel towards you, but I need to know."

"Yes, but you must know and understand I didn't mean to kill your father, I mean, I didn't even see him in the line of fire. I am so sorry I got you in this mess."

"Why did you do it? You didn't even know them."

"It's a long story, real long. And I was going to tell you but you brought it up first."

"I'm listening."

He began to explain how a father and son in his hometown had sent him off to jail for a crime the son had committed. He went on to explain how later the son had raped his sister, causing her to commit suicide. "I was deprived of my revenge on those two because they were both killed in the same car accident six months before my release. The only consolation was the accident destroyed his cherry red T-Bird."

"T-Bird?"

"Yeah, it was his pride and joy. His Daddy had given it to him for his birthday. It was the car that he was driving when he hit a fifteen-year-old girl on a bicycle. He killed her and his Daddy set me up to protect his spoiled son. Sonny let me drive it all day one Sunday all by myself. I was so stupid, I didn't even ask why? Driving that red car made me feel like I was the king of the world. I didn't even have a driver's license"

"Did he know that?"

"I'm sure he didn't care. All he wanted was my fingerprints all over the car. When I returned the car to him that night he drove it straight to the police station. I was arrested the next day. How stupid can you get, right?"

"What did you do?"

"Nothing. What could I do? I was just a trouble-making teenager.

"When I was released I made it my mission to find other Boss Carters and their sons."

"So father and Craig's death was only for revenge?" she said.

"I know it sounds awful but that's the only reason. I almost changed my mind after I met you but then Craig killed Sam McGill. Seeing those two boys without a father and knowing he would get away with killing their Dad made it easy to cancel Craig's social security number. I didn't mean to kill your father, I didn't even see him there."

"Why did you hide the gun in my car?"

"How was I to know they would go all the way to Jasper and look in your trunk? Why didn't you tell me Mr. Bob was your father?"

"I wanted to, but the time just never seemed right."

"Why did you change your name?"

"Like you it's a long story."

"Well, let me use your line...I'm listening."

"It goes back to my senior year at North Georgia College. Everything was perfect in my life. I was going to graduate in the spring and start teaching at West Fannin High School in the fall."

"What happened?"

"Just listen. I'm getting there."

"Sorry."

"It all started when I brought my roommate, Beverly Lynn, home one weekend. Craig went nuts over her. Regrettably, the feeling wasn't mutual but she did agree to go out with him only because he was my brother. Craig was enraged when he saw the relationship wasn't going the way he wanted, so he set up a special party in our cabin on the lake. I couldn't go because I had an interview with the principal for my upcoming job."

"What happened?"

"I'm getting to it, dearest... Craig had invited all his male friends, but there were only two girls, Bev and Sandi Marshall, our town slut. Craig proceeded to get Bev drunk. She had never had shine before so it was exciting for her, at first anyway. She had no way of knowing how strong it was. When she began to lose control of her actions, Craig took her to bed. She was a virgin. When Craig found this out something took him over. He encouraged all of his friends to take a turn. The disgrace of a gang rape was more than Bev could stand. She had to tell someone so she confessed everything to me on our way back to school on Sunday. When I approached my father he only laughed and asked Craig in front of me how many virgins did she make."

"Is that when you decided to leave town?"

"No. Just listen. This is harder to talk about than I thought it would be. About a month later Bev went to the school clinic because of female problems. The nurse explained to Bev that she had a venereal disease and she was required to report it to the Dean. That was more than Bev could take. That night she went to the parking lot and ran a garden hose from the exhaust pipe into the window of her car. They found her the next morning with a note asking her parents to forgive her.

"I called Father and he just laughed and said, 'I thought you were calling for her to get money for an abortion. It's good the whore is dead.' That was the last time I ever spoke to him. I don't think he thought I was serious until I had the court change my name to my mother's maiden name.

"In desperation, he tried everything to get me home. That's when he deeded our home place to me."

"How did you get to Jasper?"

"The job I have now was the position that Bev would have taken upon her graduation. I talked to the Dean at North Georgia and he made it happen."

"I understand now why the Barkleys didn't recognize who you were last fall. They seem to know you now."

"They should. After Mom died Mother Barkley treated me like the daughter she never had. My Mom and Mother Barkley were friends from childhood. Mother Barkley's love for my Mom was so strong she even tolerated Father."

"How did your Mom ever end up with Mr. Bob?"

"Big Red was Mom's...well, you figure it out...and they both worshiped each other. I think she married Father because she loved Big Red so much. I'm sure she thought Father would be just like Big Red. However, Father changed after Big Red died. The last two years Mom was alive they slept in separate bedrooms."

"Mr. Bob never knew how lucky he was to have you and your mom. He was so power hungry he missed the best thing in life—love."

"If Mom had lived maybe Craig and Father would have been better men."

"Maybe, but I don't think so!"

At exactly 5:00 p.m. Tommy came to the cell door. "I'm sorry, but it's time."

Peggy and Jim nodded their understanding. As he was getting ready to leave the guard told them that the Sheriff had granted permission for him to come back on Saturday afternoon for a couple of hours to visit. He further explained that they felt it would be best if he weren't around for the next couple of days, as the Sheriff didn't want to take any guidance from Judge Foster.

"I understand," said Jim. "I'll wait until Saturday. Thanks for all you guys have done."

"Just doing my job."

Jim left the jail and walked the two blocks to his apartment, too excited to stay home. The only thing he could think to do was visit his friend, Nick.

55
Getting Help

NICK SMILED WHEN HE SAW Jim come in. "I thought I might see you tonight."

"Set 'em up. I just had to come by and thank you for all that you've done for us."

"I did do good, didn't I?"

"Yes, sir, you did. I'll never be able to repay you."

"Yeah. You will, just tell that baby I'm its uncle."

They both laughed.

"Nick, I need to ask you a serious question."

"Shoot."

"How am I going to get Peggy out of jail?"

"That's a hard one. The only way I can think of is an appeal and I understand her lawyer has nothing on which to base one."

"What if we could find the real killer?"

"Well, that would do it, but the evidence only points to Peggy. It would take a deathbed confession, well...almost, to get her off. How do you plan on finding the killer?"

"I just don't know. Do you have any suggestions?"

"Not really."

"What if I confessed to doing it myself?"

"That's a noble idea but no judge would accept a confession from you. He would know it's only because you want to take her place."

"I can't just give up. I know she is innocent. I've just got to prove it."

"Good luck, son. I just don't know what to tell you."

"Do you think talking to State Trooper Wright could help?"

"It couldn't hurt. I think the same GBI agent that investigated Billy Bob's death investigated the murder of Craig and Mr. Bob. You know it's not too often a town loses two sheriffs in less than a month."

"I think I'll give Sam Wright a call. He's a close friend of Mike's."

The next morning he waited until he saw that Mike was alone then asked if he would come outside for a few minutes. He didn't want Mother to know he was trying to get in touch with Sam Wright.

"Sir, I'm trying to find a way to get my Peggy out of jail. Nick tells me I need to find some strong evidence before her lawyer can file an appeal. I was thinking that maybe Trooper Wright could give me some help. Do you know how I can get in touch with him?"

"Sure do. I've got a telephone numbers for both his home and work. He gave me the numbers the last time he was here."

"Do you mind calling him for me?"

"I'd love to do anything to get Margaret, I mean Peggy, out of that jail. Let's go. I'll do it right now."

"You don't mind?"

"No. Let's do it. Time's a wastin'"

Mike used the phone on his desk. Sam came on line a few seconds later.

"Sam, this is Mike Barkley."

"Is there anything wrong, sir?"

"No, the missus and I are fine. I was wondering if you might help Jim Coleman and his new wife, Peggy Taylor."

"She's married?"

"Yesterday. Jim is trying to find evidence so they can file for an appeal. We thought you might be able to help."

"Sir, you know I would do anything for you, but it seems an open and shut case. I guess I could talk to you both about it."

"Jim and I could drive down to see you if that's okay?"

"No need. Jane and I are looking to buy a cabin on the lake up there. This will give me an excuse to drive up."

"When do you think you'll come?"

"This Saturday is open for us. We could meet you at the post office around 10:00 o'clock?"

"That's great. See you then."

Saturday, 10:00 o'clock came and went. Jim was really getting worried by 11:15 a.m. and no-show.

"Do you think he changed his mind?"

"No, son, I don't. Highway 5 isn't the best road in Georgia. Saturday can be a busy day with all the farmers coming to town."

The words were hardly out of his mouth when a new Oldsmobile drove up to the post office. Sam quickly got out and ran around the car to open the door for his wife. She was busy with something in the back seat. Then they could all see what she was doing, helping a little boy from his car seat. Sam looked up at Mike, "You remember my wife, Jane?"

"Of course I do! Hello, Jane. And who is this little guy?"

"That's Michael."

"Michael, my name is Michael, too. How old are you?"

"Four," was the answer, which was accompanied by four fingers being thrust in front of Mike's face with a proud smile.

"Michael, do you like ice cream?"

Michael just nodded yes.

Mother scolded her husband, "You better ask Jane first!"

Jane replied that it was okay as he was so good on the way up, even when they were following the tractor.

"Well, Mother, let's take Jane and little Michael to the Tastee Freeze for an ice cream and let these men talk."

Jim invited Sam to his apartment and asked Sam if he would like something to drink. As Trooper Wright accepted the Coke, he invited Jim to call him Sam.

"I really appreciate you taking the time to talk with me."

"What is it that you think I can do?"

"I'm not sure, but from what I read about you in Michael Barkley's letters you can be trusted."

"Michael's letters?"

Jim explained how he had found the letters in the shed. He went on to explain to Sam about the heartbreaking troubles of Michael and Susan.

"Now I know what he meant about 'settling the score.' Where are the letters now?"

"I burned them. I was afraid the Barkleys would read them and felt they had suffered enough."

"I agree. What do you think I can do for Peggy?"

"Nick informed me that the same GBI agent that was with you the first time we met also investigated these murders."

"That's true, and that reminds me. What did Mike say your last name was?"

"Coleman. I was using Cole then because I didn't want the Barkleys to know about my past."

"Do they know now?"

"Yes, sir. I have explained it to them and what's wonderful is that it didn't make any difference with them."

"It's amazing that the truth usually hurts less than a lie, but we still lie first."

"Sam, I want the complete truth to come out now so Peggy can go free."

"What is the truth?"

"I shot them. I need you to help me prove it."

"I remember this case well. You were a suspect at first but you were the first one removed from the list. Believe me, the prosecutor tried to make you an accomplice. He dropped that approach when it was shown, not proved, you weren't in town. Are you just saying this to trade places with your wife?"

"Nick said that would be the judge's reaction."

"Nick Turner?"

"Yes. Nick is my closest friend outside of the Barkleys."

"He's a good man."

"I think so. What I need to do is prove that I came here to kill Craig on my own. I didn't even know Peggy at the time. I must prove beyond a shadow of a doubt that it was me."

"If we prove that, the judge may decide you were an accomplice and let the sentence stand. You haven't convinced me yet, much less a judge. I'm afraid you're just saying you did it so Peggy can go free. Why would you come to Blue Ridge to kill Craig?"

"It's a long story."

"Well, I'll listen. Convince me."

Jim began to give his life history to Sam, trying not to leave anything out...

Sam tried to summarize what Jim had told him. "Your father signed a pact with Boss Carter in Washington, so you went to jail instead of the son for a hit and run accident? The son raped your sister and she committed suicide. Both the father and son were killed which prevented you from getting even. So you came to Blue Ridge to get your revenge on the Fosters? Revenge by proxy was the motive. Is that it?"

"It sounds so stupid when you say it like that."

"It is stupid. Revenge never works. It never makes anyone happy, solves nothing."

"I know that now. Do you believe me?"

Well, it's hard to believe you could just make this up. Let me get GBI Agent Rodgers to make a few calls. If this proves true, I will see what I can do."

"Thanks, Sam."

"Don't thank me yet, as the best that can happen is that you trade places with Peggy. Why don't we go over to the Tastee Freeze and get some ice cream. I'm hungry."

"Then would you mind dropping me off at the jail. They said I could see Peggy this afternoon."

"Sure thing."

56
Jail Visit

AS JIM GOT OUT OF THE car, Sam said, "I'll going to make this investigation my number one priority. If Michael hadn't gotten himself killed in 'Nam I may have gotten myself in a mess like this. Believe me when I tell you that. Just be patient. These things take time, but we'll find a way to get Peggy free. Do you have a phone?"

"No, sir. Just the one in the post office."

"That's okay. I'll contact you through the Barkleys."

"Good."

"Have a nice visit. I'll do what I can."

"Thanks. That's all I can ask."

Jim was pleased to see Tommy as he walked into the jail. "Well, if it isn't Mr. Coleman," Tommy said. "Someone is really looking forward to seeing you."

"Can I see her now?"

"Sure. Until three o'clock, then she has an appointment with the Doc." Tommy then led Jim to Peggy's cell. He picked up a chair; "You'll need a chair this time because you must remain outside the cell. Sorry. Orders."

"I understand. I'm just glad I can see her. Thanks much."

He was met with a big smile from Peggy. As Tommy walked away he said, "No one will bother you two until 3:00 p.m. Be good."

They hugged each other through the bars. Then Peggy wanted to know what he'd been doing.

"Have you gone back to work?"

"I'm not working yet, but I think I'll start on Monday."

"What have you been doing?"

"Trying to find a way to get you out."

"Please don't do anything foolish. I know you didn't mean for me to be put in jail. The worst thing in the world would be for both of us to be locked up."

"Don't worry. You're innocent and that's all that matters. Mike has a state trooper friend that has volunteered to help us. It may take a while, but I've a good feeling he can help."

"That would be nice, but don't you take any chances."

"I won't."

As the doctor came in, Tommy asked Jim to leave and told him he could come back the following Saturday. After thanking the guard and saying his goodbyes to Peggy, he decided he would again go see his old friend Nick. He couldn't stand to be alone.

57
The Hospital

JIM WENT BACK TO WORK at the post office on Monday, just as he had told Peggy he would. The weeks went by slowly and he lived for his couple of hours with Peggy on Saturdays. He was really worried about her. She seemed to be getting weaker each visit. Then one Saturday as he approached the jail Tommy met him at the door.

"They took her to the hospital in Ellijay last night."

"What! Is she alright?"

"I think so. The doctor was worried about the baby."

Jim ran to the supper club, greeted Nick and said, "I need you to take me to the Ellijay hospital to see Peggy."

Nick responded calmly with, "Let me go tell Joe where I'll be."

Jim was a little nervous over Nick's speedy trip to Ellijay but didn't say a word. Clearly, Nick knew how to handle a car under high-speed conditions. Jim was surprised to see a guard outside Peggy's room. The guard stood when Nick and Jim approached, "Can I help you?"

"Yeah, Charlie, relax." The guard knew Nick and nodded. "This is the husband of the woman you are guarding. Can you let him in to talk with her?"

"I guess so."

Peggy looked weak but had a big smile for him. As he sat down on the edge of the bed he noticed she had a handcuff attached to her right leg and the bedpost.

Smiling, "I guess they are afraid you will run away."

"I guess so."

"Are you okay?"

"A little weak, but okay. The doctor just thought it would be best for the baby if I came to the hospital."

"Wow, I was so worried about you."

"I'm fine now. How did you get here?"

"Nick drove me here. He's in the hallway. I guess I need to buy a car now that you're here."

"Dummy, we have a car."

"I guess we do, the Buick! I forgot about it. Do you know where it is?"

"I'm not sure. They took it looking for evidence. Just call Charlie Robertson, the family lawyer. He'll be able to get it for you."

"I'll do that tomorrow."

"Have you heard anything from your trooper friend?"

"Not yet. I'm beginning to worry. It's been over a month."

"Be patient. You know how slow bureaucrats can be."

"I just thought Sam could cut some of that red tape."

Jim called Charlie Robertson the next day. The lawyer was shocked at the news of Peggy being married. He provided Jim with the needed information on how he could get the car. The lawyer was quick to give that information because he wanted to change the subject to something he felt was more important.

"I need to talk with you and Peggy as soon as possible. When do you think we could get together?"

"I don't know. You do know that she is in the hospital?"

"She's not in the county jail?"

"No, the doctor moved her to the hospital in Ellijay until she has the baby."

"The baby is what I want to talk with you about."

"You just tell us when you can meet with us."

"Her being in Ellijay makes it more difficult. My calendar is full until the first week of August. I could meet you both at 1:00 p.m. on August 4th."

"We'll see you then!"

Because of the hospital location instead of the jail he was able to visit with Peggy every evening instead of only on Saturday. It was a wonderful time for them both and on the August 2 they became the proud parents of a seven-pound, fourteen-ounce, seventeen-inch baby boy.

Peggy, "I would like to name him James Michael if that is okay with you."

"James Michael Coleman, President of the United States. That'll work."

They were both brought to tears when they saw how Mike and Mother treated little JM. "Look at them. If you didn't know better you'd think they were the baby's natural grandparents."

Peggy squeezed Jim's hand and whispered, "Please let them help you rear the little one."

"Don't talk like that! I'm going to get you out of here."

"I hope so, but if you don't promise me they will be part of his life."

With tears in his eyes, he whispered, "I promise."

Mike jumped up from his chair in the hospital room at just that time. "Jim! I almost forgot! Sam called. He said he had great news that he would discuss with you this weekend."

"Sweetie, did you hear that? Good news. This is our lucky day." All the while Jim knew in his heart that to trade places with Peggy was the best outcome possible, that he would very likely be tried for murder and sentenced to death. After all, killing the father was an accident, but an accident during the commission of a murder, a double-murder no matter how you sliced it.

"It certainly is. Do you know what the news could be?"

"We'll just have to wait until Saturday. Do you know when they'll release you from the hospital?"

"The doctor plans on keeping me here one more week. He doesn't feel the jail would be the best place for the baby just yet."

"Will they let you keep the baby in jail?"

"I don't think so."

"What're we going to do?"

Listening to this discussion, Mother announced, "I'll tell you what you are going to do. You and the baby are moving in with us and that's final." She stood in front of them with both hands on her hips trying to look firm.

He asked, "Are you sure?"

The Barkleys answered together, "YES!"

"Okay, only if we can pay our way."

"We agree. Now let me hold our baby boy," said Mother.

When he arrived on the fourth he found Mr. Robertson was already there.

"Jim, this is Uncle Chuck, our family lawyer. I have always called him that."

"I want you to keep calling me that," Robertson said.

"I was just telling him that they were moving me to the Atlanta federal prison next Monday morning. I can't take the baby, so you'll need to pick him up on Sunday."

He didn't know what to say.

"I'm sure Mother will help you. She'll know what to do, so just listen to her. Uncle Chuck said my father had set up a trust for his estate years ago. He was just about to tell me about it when you came in. Uncle Chuck, go on with what you were saying."

"Peggy, your father set up trust funds for you and Craig many years ago. When you changed your name to Taylor, he took the house and property out of the trust and put it in your name. At the same time he directed that all his wealth go to Craig and your children equally. He wanted to cut you out of the trust, but with Craig dead one hundred percent of the trust goes to your son."

"How much is it?"

"I'm not exactly sure, but let me just say your son is the richest kid in the county. He'll never need money. I'm currently the custodian, however, you can appoint anyone you like."

"I would like for you to continue, Uncle Chuck, if that's okay with you, Jim."

"Oh, please do. Yes. How does it work?"

"The way Bob set it up, your son will get a monthly allowance all of his life. He can get a lump sun payment for college, a car or a house. Otherwise, he is restricted from touching the principle. I was thinking we should start a check a month to your checking account for his support and maybe a lump sum check to buy all those new baby things."

"Uncle Chuck that would be wonderful. How much would you suggest?"

"I was thinking $1,000 a month for support and a $5,000 lump sum check for the basics. What do you think?"

"Jim?"

"I think it will be more than enough, but I can use the extra to pay rent to the Barkleys."

"It looks like all I need to do is to get your checking account information and do the paperwork. Jim, if you will, come by the office tomorrow around 4:00 p.m. and I'll have everything ready to sign. Please bring your marriage certificate.

"Also, I need to warn you both that Judge Foster is on the warpath. Bob's will was probated about four months ago and the judge and his wife felt they should have gotten more. That's why they wanted the baby so badly."

"What should we do?"

"Just take good care of the baby and don't give them an excuse to take him from you. I'm not worried now that I know you will be with the Barkleys. Judge Foster is afraid of Mike."

"Why is that?"

"He's afraid of any honest person, but when that person has friends, he really trembles."

"I'm leaving now."

"Here's my card, Jim.

"I guess I would like you to call me Uncle Chuck also. Just don't let your son call me Great Uncle." He laughed and, with that, was gone.

58
Good News

SATURDAY FINALLY ARRIVED AND JIM could hardly wait for Sam to show up. When Sam finally pulled up, the whole family came into the post office. The Wrights had two announcements to make. The first was that they had closed on the cabin they wanted on Blue Ridge Lake. The second was that Jane was pregnant again.

Mother was excited. "Now little James Michael will have a friend to grow up with."

"Who is James Michael?" asked Jane.

"Let's go to lunch and I'll tell you all about it."

"Great!"

Mike leaned down to Jane's son, "Michael, where do you want to eat?"

"Freeze! Freeze!"

"Tastee Freeze it is! Sam, you and Jim join us for lunch when you've finished talking business." They nodded their agreement as they headed up to Jim's apartment. Jim started asking questions before they even finished climbing the stairs.

"We verified your story. We also found new information I don't think you know about."

"Is that right?"

"Yes. Do you know why your father was so quick to agree to Mr. Carter's terms?"

"I know he was the town drunk. I just assumed Mr. Carter promised to pay his bar bills."

"He did do that. However, your father had a much bigger problem. He owed a $30,000 gambling debt. Mr. Carter knew your father gambled so he had his lawyer pick up your father's IOUs around the county. When the Carters were killed, his lawyer grew a conscience. Actually, he was forced into it. When the county sheriff opened Mr. Carter's safe there were a lot of damaging documents that could be used against the lawyer. He decided it would be best if he agreed to a complete disclosure to keep him out of jail."

"You told Mike you had good news. Is that it?"

"Not all of it. Mr. Carter had his lawyer draw up a detailed contract with your father, which outlined what he wanted him to do. I'm sure it was just to scare your father into compliance and they never meant anyone to see it. The good news is that the judge and prosecutor that sent you to jail went to the Governor of the State personally and had your record expunged."

"What does that mean?"

"Not only did the Governor pardon you, he had any paperwork that referred to your case destroyed. It's as if it never happened."

"When did all this take place?"

"About six months after your release. They couldn't let you know because you disappeared. It was like you dropped off the face of the earth. They even screened driver's licenses that were issued each year in an effort to contact you. The clerk that has been following this case wrote everyone with no results. They finally decided you left the state, so they closed the case."

"That's good news? I don't have a record. How is that going to help Peggy?"

"I'm not sure it will."

"Sam, do you believe I killed Craig?"

"No, Jim. I can't say that I do. I want to, but the more I get to know you, the more I feel you don't have it in you to kill in cold blood."

"Sam, if I can't convince you, how am I ever going to be able to convince a judge and jury?"

"What we need now is to find details that only the killer would know that do not involve Peggy."

"Can you get copies of the transcripts?"

"I already have. They are public record, but those only have what was brought out in court. I also have a copy of the case files. There is information in those that was never made public. If we are going to make a case for an appeal we need to tie these pieces of evidence to someone else."

"Sam, it looks like I will need to convince you I did it before we will ever make a case a judge would listen to."

"That would be a good starting point."

"Let me give you some facts I know that might just convince you I'm who I say I am."

"Shoot! Oh, I'm sorry."

"I need for you to take me seriously."

"I'll try but I'm telling you it will be hard."

"Why don't you start a list and you can compare it with the case files later. First, when Craig was shot, Mr. Campbell, the scoutmaster, was there to collect a $2,000 check from Mr. Bob. The sniper position in the woods had an old red shirt, a .243 empty shell and some of the limbs had been pruned away. Oh, and the bullet struck Craig two inches below his badge."

Sam's face turned white. "You really did shoot them."

"I shot Craig. Mr. Bob was an accident."

"The law still calls that murder."

"I understand that. Now how do we prove it and not involve Peggy?"

"That will be hard to prove. I think the revenge by proxy motive will be the way to go. We need to make sure they don't think you knew about your pardon. Where were you for the last couple of years?"

"All over the state."

"You didn't leave Georgia?"

"No. I would only stay in one place for four to six months."

Nervously Sam asked, "Is the Foster family the first one you took your revenge on?"

"No. There was another one."

"Good. I don't mean good you killed them, but good if we can prove you did another one. Then we should be able to prove you did this one without involving Peggy."

"Now we're talking!"

"I need everything you can remember about the other killing."

"It was in Dexter, Georgia more than two years ago. It was another father and son. Bart Woods and his son, Junior. They were both killed with a .30-06 Springfield rifle. An Army rifle converted into a hunting rifle, in other words. The son was shot at the top of the stairs and the father was killed in the living room. He was found with the rifle in his hand. Over $200,000 dollars was missing."

"You talk about this as if it was just a game."

"In a way it was, a revenge game. I knew my life was over and I wanted revenge. When I couldn't get revenge on the people that had destroyed my life I began to look for people that were destroying other people's lives. You know, finding them was easy. I identified the Fosters in less than an hour after getting off the bus. Parasites like the Fosters are all over the South."

"So you took it upon yourself to do God's work?"

"I didn't think of it like that, I just wanted revenge. I didn't want to believe my life would be wasted."

"Doesn't the Good Book say something about, 'Vengeance is mine, saith the Lord?' "

"Absolutely. I now understand what that means! If I can just take Peggy's place, I'll be happy. I hope God is not using the possible execution of Peggy as my punishment for trying to take his place."

"I don't think God does things like that."

"If I had only known she was Mr. Bob's daughter, it would've been different."

"Are you sure?"

"Oh yeah. I was already having doubts about the revenge thing, then Craig killed Sam McGill."

"I heard about that. Didn't he attack Craig first?"

"Yeah, after he fucked his wife in front of his little boy!"

"You know I'm starting to believe Craig was an asshole."

"Starting to believe? Hey, with a capital A."

"Jim, I'm working with the GBI on the investigation. Because the case is closed we must do it on our own time and expense. You need to know it may take months or years to get the evidence we need."

"How can we speed the process up?"

"We could hire a private investigator, but that would be expensive."

"Let me worry about the expenses. I've got money. Why don't you go down to the car and I'll meet you there."

When Sam left, he moved to his hiding place and quickly counted out $5,000. Getting into the car, he handed it all to Sam.

"Is this part of the $50,000 they said Peggy had blackmailed from her father?"

"No. I have all that money in a safe place. Not here."

"You blackmailed him also?"

"Afraid so."

"I'll never understand you."

"I'm not sure I do."

59

Baby's New Home

"What time are you and Mother coming to pick up JM?" asked Peggy.

"About 1:00 p.m., right after they get home from church."

"That'll be good. You know I never went to church. Father didn't believe in God. Do you?"

"If you had asked me that two years ago, I would have said no. Now I can say without doubt, yes."

"Good. Rear our child the right way."

"Don't talk that way. I've got a feeling with Sam's help you will be free one day soon."

"That would be nice, however, I couldn't be any happier than I am right now."

It was about 2:00 p.m. when they got to the hospital. The word had leaked to the press that Peggy was being transferred to Atlanta Federal. A hundred or so reporters were out front and the federal guards had taken control. He was not allowed to see Peggy—the only reason he was allowed entry at all was to get the baby.

Jim was escorted out a side door so the reporters would not see him leave. Just before he left the building he asked the man who looked to be in charge of the operation when he could see Peggy again.

"Visitation is the last Saturday of the month. Now leave," was his curt reply.

Mother cried all the way home. Mike kept telling her, "Mother, you need to stop crying. You're upsetting the baby."

"I'm sorry, Mike. I'm trying to stop. It's just so awful."

At first, chaos had taken over the Barkley's house with the new baby but slowly things began to settle down. With all the love and attention, JM was growing like a weed. He smiled, rolled over, began crawling, then walking—all the new things a baby does that wraps adults around their little fingers.

Jim made monthly trips to see Peggy. She was not allowed to see her son except on his birthday. Jim took JM to see Peggy on the little one's second birthday when he got a call from Sam.

"What's the news, Sam?"

"We finally received permission to look at the case in Dexter. Everything you said was true, but I'm afraid I have bad news. They ruled it a murder/suicide."

"What?!" Jim yelled.

"The father shot the son for stealing $250,000 and then turned the gun on himself. All the evidence points that way."

"Did you tell them I confessed to the killing?

"Yes, we did. We pointed out your reasons for killing them but they had complete power over the money and politics of the town and county. They abused this power and walked on the people of the community. The worst thing was no matter what they did they would never be charged with any legal wrongdoing. The Woods felt they were above the law, in fact acted as if they were the law.

"What did the people say about that?"

"The people we talked with were quick to tell us how the Woods had abused the law and the people of the community."

"Then what's the problem?"

"The worst thing is the community is glad the Woods are dead and the case is closed and they don't want it brought up again. One of the officials said it best. 'If he did do it, he did us all a great favor. We want you to drop it. Let sleeping dogs lie!'"

"Is there nothing you can do then, about Peggy, I mean?"

"I don't think so. I'm afraid with what little we have now the GBI and Governor will feel the same."

"Sam we're running out of time."

"I know! This may not be the best time and I hate to ask, but we are out of money. Walter and I have tried to do everything the cheapest way we could however we still need that private investigator if we are going to find what we need in time."

"For God's sake stop cutting corners! I told you I've got money. How much do you need? Forget that! I'll send you $100,000 by certified mail on Monday. When that's gone let me know."

"Is that the money I think it is?"

"Yes, but can you think of a better way to spend it, Sam?"

"Not really! Jim, I'm beginning to believe Dexter is a dead end. I'm almost afraid to ask this, but is there another family where you straightened out there problems?"

"Yes the Stricklands."

"I was afraid that would be your answer. Where and how many?"

"Hinesville, Georgia. Next to Ft. Stewart."

"Is that near Savannah?"

"Just a little southwest."

"I know the place."

"It was twin brothers, Wayne and Blaine Strickland. Their father had made a fortune in forestry and the pitch business."

"Don't give me any more details. I will see what Walter and I can find out."

"How long is this going to take? I can't wait another six months."

"Oh, no. We will have something in a couple of weeks. Jane has already made plans to have another family picnic in two weeks."

"The Barkleys will love that."

"They seem happy."

"You should see them alone with JM. No kid has ever been loved more."

"That's easy to see."

60

New Postal Worker

THE TWO WEEKS WENT BY quicker than Jim had expected. Now that he was a full-fledged postman he worked extra hard to impress Mike. Seeing what he was doing, Mike called him out in front of the other postal workers, "Jim, you don't need to do everything in one day. They pay us for five days for a reason." Then he gave out his famous belly laugh. The other postmen laughed and patted him on the back. At that moment Jim realized he had truly been accepted into the post office family. He still had the warm feeling inside as he drove his little family to the Wright's cabin.

Just like any normal Southern family after 30 minutes each broke away to their own interests. At this time Jim and Sam walked down to the lake where they could talk.

"Do you have any better news this week?"

"Not really. In fact, we have run up against two major obstacles."

"What are they?"

"First, the fact that all the cases are closed. They were closed because of a logical solution. Add to that the fact that no one wants the cases reopened because it could cause major ripples in some of these small towns, new evidence, new witnesses and an increased cause for doubting the system. But that's not the major obstacle."

"Then what is?"

"If what you say is true, then there has been a serial killer in Georgia for the past four years and the State of Georgia knew nothing about it. That would be a major embarrassment to the Governor, the GBI and a lot of other folks. Are you getting the drift?"

"I see what you mean. Politicians do not like to be embarrassed. What can I do? We can't let Peggy die just to make these people feel comfortable!"

"Give me some more details. Maybe I can find something that the prosecutor can use to reopen the case anyway."

"What do you have now?"

"The leaders of small towns were killed one family per year. All were killed with a Springfield .30-06 rifle and 180-grain bullets. We can only prove you were in the community two of these times."

"That's it?"

"Well, some of the other information doesn't help much. They owned the town. They walked on the people. They were never charged for any legal wrongdoing. Jim, my biggest problem with the prosecutor is you."

"Me?"

"Yes. It bothers him if you were smart enough to do all the other killings, why didn't you see you were setting up Peggy? He truly feels you are just wanting to take her place. Can you see it from his point of view?"

"I didn't have a clue that Peggy was Mr. Bob's daughter! I only saw her as the woman that I loved"

"How do we prove that?"

"Mike, Mother and Nick can tell them."

"Their testimony would be hearsay at best."

"We need some physical proof if we are going to get a new trial."

"How about this? In all the other cases the rifle did not have a scope."

"That's true, but what does that prove?"

"Well, the rifle in Peggy's trunk had a scope still mounted."

"How did you know that?"

"Sam! I put it there. Remember? When are you really going to believe I killed Craig and Mr. Bob?"

"I keep trying but over the last few months we have become friends. I'm having a hard time believing you were ever as vindictive as you described."

"Trust me, I was. I only wanted revenge and money—and in that order."

"What are you telling me about the other rifles?"

"That is a very special scope and requires a special mount. If you will check all the other rifles you'll find the scope from Peggy's rifle will fit them perfectly."

"Why didn't you take the scope off the rifle in Peggy's trunk?"

"This was my last job. Didn't have time. I wanted to start a new life. I didn't need the scope anymore. If it will help I can tell you the name of the man that mounted it."

"I'll check the other weapons. What's the gunsmith name? This may be just the evidence we need."

"I don't know his last name. His first name is Kurt. His shop was Kurt's Gun and Supplies, in Atlanta. That's all I can remember. Oh, yeah, he couldn't convert mine quick enough so he just traded me one of his."

"Quick enough? Did you tell him you needed to kill a man ASAP?"

"You have the sickest sense of humor. No, I told him I wanted it for hunting season."

"Did you go hunting?"

"No, stupid, I just told him that!"

"Okay! Okay relax I'm just funning with you."

"I'm sorry. It's just I'm so afraid we've going to run out of time."

"Cheer up. I think we have something Walter can work with now. Be patient. We will be as fast as we can. But you know when you are working with small towns or county officials; if they feel pressured or rushed they get slower or even stop until they feel they are in charge again. That's the way of bureaucrats. Things get done but at their pace."

"I understand. But please keep them moving."

"We will!"

61

Execution Postponed

THE PHONE RANG LATE ONE evening at the Barkley home. Mike answered it on the second ring, "Well it's about time you called. Jim has been going crazy with worry because you haven't called. Do you have good news? When are you coming to Blue Ridge? Saturday at your cabin would be wonderful. I'll tell Mother. Hold on, I'll get Jim. Jim, it's Sam...says the new county judge has gotten Peggy's execution postponed. Isn't that wonderful?"

Jim ran to the phone. "Peggy's execution is postponed? Does that mean we got a new trial?"

Mike could hear the disappointment in his voice. "Right. We can talk in more detail on Saturday. Around noon, we'll see you then. Thanks, bye."

Mike stood there with a question on his face. He was too polite to ask. Jim felt he should know so he quietly said, "Sam said the new judge, a Judge Colwell from Blairsville, requested the postponement. But he didn't request a new trial."

"Son, it's good Peggy has Judge Colwell on her side."

"Why is that? What do you mean?"

"Ever since Judge Foster beat him in an election years ago there has been a feud between them. The reason was that Mr. Bob bought the election. Nothing would make Judge Colwell happier than putting egg on Judge Foster's face. If Sam and that GBI fellow can find anything, I'm sure Judge Colwell will use it. I can feel things turning in our favor. I can feel it."

"That's good, isn't it?" He asked with hope on his face once again.

"I think so."

Saturday noon arrived with everyone comfortable on the front porch of the Wright's cabin. An outsider seeing the gathering would have thought it was a typical family reunion. In a way it was. In most families the common bond is blood. In this family the common bond was Michael Barkley. Even though he had been dead for years the bond was still as strong as blood kin.

After a couple of hours, Jim and Sam found a place they could quietly talk. Jim was quick to ask how he was coming with his investigation.

"We talked to Kurt. He remembered you and the scope. This is the first hard evidence we've found."

"That's good isn't it?"

"It's a start but this by itself would be only enough to prove you were an accomplice to the killings."

"What about the other rifles?"

"That's our next step."

"Good! I'm starting to feel we're on the right tract now."

"Me too! I'll give you a call at the end of the month."

62
Brotherhood

TWO MONTHS LATER SOMEONE ASKED for Jim at the front of the post office. Jim hurried to the front and saw Sam. "What happened to the I'll-call-you at the end of the month stuff?"

"I'm so sorry. We ran into some problems."

"You should have called anyway. How long has it been?"

"Too long. I'm sorry. Every week I thought in a few days I would have good news for you. It didn't happen and the weeks slipped by."

"Well, tell me what this big problem is."

"We can't find the rifles."

"What do you mean you can't find the rifles? Aren't they locked up in some evidence room or something?"

"That's what we thought. The problem is that the cases were closed and the property went to the next of kin."

"Do you know who that is?"

"Not really. Our PI pissed off the local police and they can't seem to locate the chain of evidence logs."

"Doesn't the PI understand local protocol?"

"He has a masters degree now! Is there someplace we can talk in private?"

"Sure let's go outside and use the bench. No one will be there this time of day."

"When we talked with Kurt about the rifle he mentioned that you came in with Billy Bob Foster."

"That's right. So?"

"My occupation forces me to ask. Did you have anything to do with his death?"

"If I said yes, would it help to get Peggy out of jail?"

"I don't think so. First of all, you'd have no motive to kill him. Would you?"

"What about the fact that he killed Susan?"

"Susan?"

"Yes, Michael's wife. He tried to blackmail her into having sex with him and she snapped and came at him with a knife. Sam, he shot her four times."

Sam just couldn't believe what he was hearing.

"Are you sure?"

"You need to talk to Nick about it. He knows the whole story. I just know what Billy Bob bragged about doing."

"Jim, you just don't know how this news hurts me. You need to know that Michael and I were almost like brothers. When I arrived in 'Nam, I'd only been a captain two weeks. Michael was the senior warrant officer. We worked together daily. All the other warrant officers had the highest respect for him. If it hadn't have been for Michael, WOPA (Warrant Officer Protective Association) would have run my flight platoon instead of me. I made a few mistakes initially and Michael took me aside, like a little brother, and explained to me the ramifications of my quick decisions. He made alternative suggestions on how to get the job done using creative leadership. I may have outranked him in the military, but I was the student. He really did the hard work of running my platoon and I reaped the rewards of high reports and medals. So, after what you've told me about Susan's death, if you did shoot Billy Bob I owe you big time. I want you to know I will never ask anything about him again."

"Michael must have been a wonderful man. I wish I had had the opportunity to have known him."

"You do know him. His name is Mike. They were like two peas in a pod. Michael asked for my help and I regret I didn't take the request more seriously. I'm taking your request for help with Peggy very seriously and I will do whatever I can to get her released. I want you to understand it bothers me that if things work out, I will be sacrificing your freedom for Peggy's. I'm not sure I'm comfortable with that."

"Be comfortable. What's that old saying, 'When you do the crime, be prepared to do the time?' I am prepared and want to do it. What's our next step?"

"Truthfully, I'm running out of ideas. But we have got to find those guns."

"Why don't you have the PI offer a reward for the rifles? $1,000 for information leading to their whereabouts and $500 for the rifle."

"You know, that might work. Why didn't I think of that?"

"Basically, Sam, you're still a cop."

"Are you going to hold that against me?"

"No way! That's the only reason I feel we may actually get this mess straightened out. How are you doing for money?"

"We still have a little, but not enough to cover the rewards."

"I'll send you another $50,000 by certified mail tomorrow."

"Good. I'll put the PI on getting leaflets printed and distributed in both Dexter and Hinesville. This should break the logjam. I'll give you a call one way or the other in two weeks."

"Can I depend on that?"

"I promise. Good news or bad."

"Hopefully it will be good news. You had lunch yet?"

"My treat."

63
The Rifles

THE PHONE RANG AT THE Barkleys and Jim picked it up on the third ring. He immediately recognized Sam's voice.

"What you got for me?"

"Some good news."

"That means you've got some bad news, right?"

"Yeah."

"Give me the good first."

"The reward worked. We found the rifle in Hinesville. Apparently one of the deputies took it when no one claimed it. The sheriff's office has been covering up that fact."

"That's great. Was it like I said?"

"Yes. Some of the markings were there. The problem is the deputy had a gunsmith mount another scope on it and the old mount sites were damaged."

"What does that mean?"

"It'll be hard to prove that your scope could mount on this weapon. There're only two attachment points left. We'll need the other rifle to compare with this one. Another good point, or bad, depending upon how you look at it; you have now convinced Walter you are a serial killer. His professional pride is killing him. He knows you are what you say you are, but like you, he can't prove it. That tells me we are on the right track. If we convinced Walter, it can't take too much more to convince a judge. We just have to find that other rifle."

"How's it look?"

"Not very good, Jim. We haven't had one nibble in Dexter. In fact, everyone hated the Woods so much they now refuse to even talk about them."

"Increase the reward. $5,000. $1,000 for the gun. No, make that $10,000 for the gun. That should get something going."

"God, I hope so."

"We've lost so much time I'm scared to death for Peggy. She can't stay on death row forever."

"Ten thousand should get us the gun. I'll call you when we've got it. Bye."

64

The Pardon

IT WAS ALMOST 9:00 P.M. when the phone rang. Jim answered and immediately Sam began to apologize for calling so late.

"I wanted to let you know your idea of increasing the reward has shook up the Dexter community."

"Did you get the rifle?"

"No, but every person in the county that owns a Springfield .30-06 has called trying to say that their weapon is the one we want."

"That sounds great."

"Yeah. We're excited. In fact Walter is so excited he thinks it's time to take the information and evidence we have to the Governor and request a complete pardon for Peggy. He feels we can prove that a serial killer killed the Fosters. Before we make that big a move we wanted your approval. What do you think?"

"How risky is it? If he says no, does it stop us from asking later?"

"We don't think so but if we don't ask he can't say yes."

"When do you want to do it?"

"Walter says it will take him at least two weeks to get all the legal papers and work done. Add another week to get an appointment with the Governor."

"Do we need a lawyer?"

"It would be helpful. Who were you thinking of? Peggy's lawyer?"

"Yeah. I'm sure Uncle Chuck would want to be involved in getting her released. I'll give him a call first thing in the morning and set up a planning meeting with you and Walter. When would be a good time?"

"My best guess would be Thursday or Friday."

"Fine, I'll check to make sure that time is good for him and get back with you."

"Thanks, Sam. You've made my day."

Months later as the Barkleys were driving home, Mother asked, "Do you think it would be wrong to give JM a birthday party?"

"No, I don't. You know you are only three once."

"Should we have the party at home or someplace else?"

"Let's do it at the Tastee Freeze and invite everyone in town!"

"Mike, you're crazy. But it does sound like fun."

"Let's talk to Jim when he gets back from Atlanta."

"How much longer will he be there?"

"Only a couple more days."

Mother said, "I've got a great idea! Let's talk to Jane and Sam. We could invite them to bring Michael and Sarah. What do you think about us all going to a picnic on top of Hogback?"

"A wonderful idea! Peggy has always said that Hogback was her favorite place in the whole world. This time of year it's beautiful. Mother, that's absolutely perfect. That's what we're going to do. I can taste the fried chicken and your potato salad now!"

"This family needs to start celebrating the good things that life has given us!"

"I agree."

While unloading the car in the driveway, Mother asked, "Mike, would you check to see if we got today's newspaper?"

When Mike opened the door, Mother could see he was pale as a ghost. He was holding the Atlanta Journal and staring at the headline.

"What is it, Mike? What's wrong?"

Mike's voice trembled as he read the words aloud, words that were final and inescapable, "The Warden at the Atlanta Federal Prison pronounced Margaret Taylor Coleman legally dead at 12:01 a.m."

Printed in the United States
64964LVS00012B/43-48